# Bound Angel

## Felicity Heaton

# HER ANGEL: BOUND WARRIORS SERIES

Dark Angel
Fallen Angel
Warrior Angel
Bound Angel

Find out more at: www.felicityheaton.com

# CHAPTER 1

The angel was back.

Rook stood on the precipice of a spire of black rock, staring at the shadowy horizon in the direction of the Devil's fortress, not seeing its spiky towers. Not seeing the cragged lands around him that shimmered in the heat. Not seeing the fiery rivers that forked like lightning across the obsidian earth below him, illuminating the endless cavern of Hell.

Not seeing anything.

His gaze was turned inwards, focused on the strange sensation that swirled inside him whenever the angel entered Hell and dared to leave the plateau overlooking the bottomless pit.

Rook had noticed it during their second encounter, when he had spotted the black-haired and onyx-winged angel scouting lands he had no right surveying.

It was one thing for Heaven to have a contingent of angels posted on the plateau, where a silvery pool recorded the history of the mortal realm.

It was another thing entirely for one of his foul breed to leave that place and fly where he didn't belong, trampling all over the Devil's territory.

Three times since then, Rook had dispatched the First Battalion to drive the male back.

Three times since then, the angel had gone quietly, retreating not just to the plateau but to a portal he could open between Hell and the mortal realm.

Which meant he was powerful.

Was that the reason Rook could sense him?

His eyes slipped shut and he inhaled slowly, filled his lungs with the sweet air of Hell and exhaled it all again, centring himself at the same time. The sensation grew stronger, swirled more violently inside him. Not in his gut, but behind the breastplate of his scarlet-edged black armour.

As he focused on it, it grew stronger still, setting him on edge. He shunned the unsettling emotion, refusing to let the angel rattle him again.

The last time the angel had entered Hell, Rook's commander had been busy. Rook had led the men in his stead, flying to meet the angel head on, determined to drive the angel out of Hell.

Determined to prove himself worthy of his position in the First Battalion, both to his commander and to the Devil.

There were rumours the commander was falling out of favour. Rook was damned if another would take his place as leader of the First Battalion when he had spent centuries working towards seizing control of the elite legion.

When he had found the intruder, the male had dared to address him directly and calmly despite the threat of facing a hundred of Hell's most powerful angels.

He had mentioned a witch and something about helping her.

It had given Rook pause, and that had left him cold, and furious. He had driven the angel out of Hell, pursuing him right to the plateau to ensure he left, because no creature of Heaven could sway him from his path.

The fiend had been trying to lure him from Hell. Rook was sure of it.

He just wasn't sure why the male wanted him to leave the realm of shadows and fire that was his home, his entire world.

His left hand fell to the red-edged obsidian vambrace that protected his right forearm and he clutched it as a different feeling rolled through him, one he despised. It always left him off balance, filling him with uncertainty—both about himself and the realm he loved so much.

He focused to purge the sensation before it took hold. If he let it seize him, questions would flood his mind, slipping through his fingers like smoke, fleeing before they had even fully formed. He needed his mind in the present and sharp as a blade with the angel in his territory. He couldn't allow the tangled flow of questions and indistinct thoughts to strip him of his awareness today, weakening him.

The angel was coming.

To lure him through the portal into the mortal realm? For what purpose?

To kill him?

It wouldn't be the first time that an angel of Heaven had lured one serving the Devil away from this realm to kill them, forcing them to return to Heaven.

Rook had no interest in dying, so he wasn't interested in the angel or anything he had to say.

The bastard was persistent though.

He had returned quicker this time, and seemed to be heading swiftly in Rook's direction, as if he knew where he stood.

Impossible.

Hell was vast, blurred into shadows as far as the eye could see, no matter how far he flew. It was filled with angels like him too, ones who served the Devil, and countless demons. It shouldn't be possible for the male to single him out in the web of signatures.

Yet when Rook opened his eyes, a speck formed on the horizon, a glint of gold in a sea of red and black.

He rolled his head, stretching his neck, and flexed his fingers as he lowered his hands to his hips. He rested his left hand on the black hilt of the scarlet blade hanging at his waist and extended his crimson wings. His gaze darted to them and he swiftly checked his feathers were lined up perfectly and his wings were ready for when he needed them. He casually furled them against his back as the angel drew closer, so they brushed the pointed slats of armour that protected his hips and the backs of his greaves.

His heart beat harder, muscles coiling beneath his skin as he waited.

*Waited.*

For a moment, it looked as if the angel would fly straight past him and then he diverted course, banking to his right and descending towards a flat section of the hill that rose to Rook's left.

The male landed gracefully, neatened his ponytail with a steady hand, and gave a few more beats of his onyx wings before allowing them to settle against his back. He turned towards Rook, lifted his head and pinned him with bright blue eyes that glowed against the darkness of Hell.

Rook refused to move from his spire of rock.

He glared down at the male, his fingers tightening around the hilt of his sword. "Not learned your lesson yet?"

The male regarded him silently, no trace of emotion crossing his features.

Rook growled through his fangs at him as all of his teeth sharpened and turned crimson in response to the anger that blazed in his veins.

The angel was trespassing, should at least have the decency to harbour even the smallest flicker of fear or doubt in his eyes. The way the angel treated Hell as if he was allowed to roam it freely, without consequence, had riled Rook the moment he had met him centuries ago. It had only irritated him more each time he had seen the angel after that.

Coupled with the fact this angel seemed able to withstand the Devil's voice, even went as far as challenging his master at times, throwing curses back at him, the male really pissed him off.

Rook rolled his shoulders and didn't hold back the rage pouring through his veins. He let it flow over him and carry him away, stoked it as he narrowed his now-crimson eyes on the male. The angel dared to stand before him, to linger in his presence without fear. Worse than that, he dared to do it unarmed.

The bastard was taunting him.

Rook wasn't going to stand for it.

The male thought himself powerful, believed himself able to handle Rook without a weapon to aid him.

Rook would show him what a mistake all his beliefs were.

His bones lengthened as hunger to eradicate the angel that had become his nemesis rolled through him, born of a desire to return his focus to claiming command of the First Battalion. A shadow swept over his skin, turning it black, and he growled through his all-sharp teeth. The angel appeared to move further away as Rook continued to grow, shifting into his demonic form.

As the crimson rolled down Rook's feathers like blood to drip from their tips, leaving them onyx, the angel reacted at last.

A flicker of something that looked like remorse danced across his blue eyes as they shifted to Rook's wings, as he watched the feathers fall away to reveal the dark dragon-like form they concealed.

Rook spread those wings and bared his teeth at the male as he drew the weapon hanging from his waist. It transformed as he swept his hand over it, going from a short crimson blade to a mighty broadsword, one capable of cleaving the angel in two with a single stroke.

The angel's eyes leaped to it as Rook wrapped his other hand around the elongated hilt and brought it down before him, a pounding urge to relieve the angel of his head rushing through him.

That remorse lingered in their blue depths.

Rook snarled again.

Fear should be the only emotion the angel was feeling. Sheer terror that his life was about to end now that Rook stood before him in his demonic guise, a form that granted him more power than he commanded in his angelic one.

When another emotion joined the remorse in the angel's eyes, Rook launched from the spire of rock with such force it shattered. A sound like the crack of lightning echoed around Hell as he shot towards the angel, determined to end him.

Because no one pitied him.

He was strong. He beat his wings. He had worked his way through the ranks of the Devil's angels. He beat them harder. He had commanded the Second Battalion, led them in wars against Heaven and in the mortal world. He beat them harder still. He was second in command in the First Battalion, close to his goal of leading the most fearsome legion in Hell.

He drew his sword back, his gaze focused on his target.

He would prove it to this angel. Right here and right now.

The last feelings the male would know were pity and remorse for questioning his strength.

He swung hard, his aim true, and grinned as his blade closed in on the angel's throat.

"Rook."

That word, uttered in a calm way that was such a contrast to the maelstrom of emotion whirling inside him, halted him in the air as surely as a sword through his heart might have. He stared down at his chest, sure he would find a blade piercing it as pain rolled outwards from the centre of it, had his hands trembling and broadsword rattling just inches from the angel.

"What the *fuck*?" he snarled and beat his wings, shot backwards to regroup and get the sudden flood of feelings that poured through him under control.

They swirled and collided, all of them birthed by hearing this angel utter his name. He understood none of them, not where they came from or what they meant, couldn't untangle the web of them no matter how hard he tried.

Rook swept his blade down by his side and growled as he realised the angel was playing him for a fool. It was all a trick. An elaborate one. The bastard wanted to lure him into a trap. How many others like Rook had this angel killed and returned to Heaven, taking their free will from them?

He served the Devil because he wanted to serve him.

This realm was his home, his entire world.

The hilt of his sword clanked against his armour as he instinctively reached for his forearm in response to that and the niggling sensation that something else had been his entire world once.

Heaven?

He shunned that thought. Even if somewhere else had been his entire world once, Hell was that place for him now. Nothing would change that.

"I know you." The angel took a step towards him, the fires of Hell reflecting off the gold edges of his black armour that moulded to his upper chest, forearms and shins, and the pointed strips that protected his hips. "I know you, Rook. It was long ago, many centuries now. I thought you dead... foolish, I see that now. Or perhaps you did die... a part of you died and it led to you serving this place."

Rook spread his wings and beat them again, not to move away from the angel but to hold a position in the air above him. He wouldn't run from this male, wouldn't allow his poisonous words to taint his heart and dissolve his strength. They were all lies, designed to weaken him.

"Any angel could discover my name," he spat and narrowed his crimson eyes on the male. "Don't think yourself clever in your approach to attempting to be my downfall."

"Downfall?" The male's lips curled slightly, a rueful edge to his smile. "Your downfall is not me, and it is not now. It happened all those centuries ago… the night you chose to serve this wretched realm."

Rook growled at that, flashing his fangs. "You know nothing of me… your realm is the wretched one, and your kind are foul fiends, determined to place my kind in Heaven's shackles again."

"I do not want to kill you, Rook." The male shook his head, a slight frown furrowing his brow. "It would defeat the purpose of my being here."

There was a glimmer of something in the male's blue eyes that said he had considered killing him at one point though. For what reason? And why hadn't he gone through with that plan?

"Why are you here then?" Rook let his demonic form fade away to conserve his strength. It was taxing to use it, wore him out even when he was in Hell, a place that was his home. His entire world. His fingers twitched with a need he suppressed. "If not to taunt me and lure me somewhere you can murder me?"

"I needed to speak with you."

Him in particular?

"So speak, and then leave." He swept his hand back up his blade to shorten it, but kept it out, gripped at his side in case he needed it.

He tried to deny the curiosity growing inside him, but its grip on him was as fierce as his on his sword, and he found himself wanting to hear what had brought the angel into Hell and to him.

"The witch—"

"Again with this witch?" Rook cut him off.

Why did the angel keep bringing up the female?

His free hand twitched.

He ignored it.

"She needs your help, Rook." The male took another step forwards, closer to him, and tilted his head up, causing his ponytail to slip from the shoulder of his black armour.

Armour that so closely matched Rook's own. Strange how an angel who served Heaven could be given such dark armour and wings. It hardly seemed fitting. All the angels who worked near the pool were of this male's kind though. Rook had only seen one mediator, angels with white wings, in his time. That male had come with this one a few months ago, and Rook had watched them until the Devil had grown furious and had ordered him away from them.

"You help her. I'm not interested." He went to turn away as a pressing need to leave built inside him.

The Devil exerting his will on him.

He felt it as a tug in his chest, one that had him wanting to move to a distance and call on his legion. He didn't need to call to them. They were already coming. He could feel it in his blood. Soon, this angel would face the strongest battalion serving Hell.

This time, Rook wouldn't let the angel flee.

"I cannot find her." The angel shifted his foot forwards, looking as if he might risk another step, and then clenched his fists at his sides and loosed a black curse. "Listen to me, Rook. She needs *you*. Only you can find her. I believe that."

Rook chuckled at that. "You believe it? I am expected to go along with your beliefs? I don't think so. I recommend you leave now."

The male stared him down, his blue eyes sober. "You believed in her once."

He froze again, the collision of feelings he couldn't grasp sending his mind swirling. Had he known the witch the angel spoke of? His free hand twitched, and this time he didn't hold it back. He brushed his fingers over the raised crimson crossed axes on his vambrace and down over the skull below them.

He searched his memories and found none of a witch. He had never met one of her kind before. The angel was mistaken.

Dark words rang in his head, his order clear. Make the male leave now or face the consequences of disobedience.

Rook swept his palm down the length of his blade again, transforming it back into his crimson broadsword. He beat his scarlet feathered wings, focused his mind and readied himself.

"Will you listen to me?" the angel barked. "Do not listen to him. He wants you here for some reason. Rook, you *must* listen to me."

He growled, baring his sharp teeth, and gripped his sword in both hands. "I know no witch. I have never met one of her kind. I don't have to listen to you because you mean to deceive me."

"Fine, Rook." The male rose to his full height, tipping his chin up as his blue eyes brightened, glowing in the low light. He held his hands out in front of him and twin curved golden blades appeared in them. "We will do this the hard way."

Rook readied his own sword.

The angel unleashed his black wings, twisted away from him and beat them, hurling a wave of dust at Rook as he shot into the distance.

Rook snarled and gave chase, his wings beating furiously as he fought to catch up. He was damned if he would let the angel escape again. This time, the male was going down. He would capture the creature and present him to the Devil, and his master would recognise his strength and skill.

The position of next commander of the First Battalion would be secured.

Everything he had ever wanted in life would be his.

His wrists burned and he grunted as a wave of fire encircled them, chasing around them beneath his vambraces and searing his bones.

It was all he wanted.

This realm was his everything.

He gritted his teeth against the ribbons of fire as they blazed hotter.

His entire world.

He squeezed his eyes shut.

A feminine voice echoed in the darkness, cutting through the pain.

It reached to him and wrapped him in comforting arms that stole it all away, left him drifting in the shadows, feeling light inside.

*"I'll be with you forever."*

Heat streaked down his cheeks as tremendous pain welled up inside him, agony he couldn't contain.

He threw his head back and roared.

A single thought crystallised as he emptied his lungs in a desperate attempt to purge the pain that was tearing him to pieces, threatening to consume and destroy him.

The owner of that voice was his entire world.

It shattered as quickly as it had formed.

Rook frowned down at his wrists as he beat his wings to keep him in the air. The breeze from them cooled his face for some reason. He lifted his free hand and brushed his fingers across the wetness on his cheeks, canted his head and studied it as he brought them away.

It meant nothing.

He shifted his gaze from them and fixed it on the retreating angel.

A male who would be his prize and would secure his elevation in the ranks.

He flapped his wings and shot after him, because achieving the position of commander of the First Battalion and the power it would gain him was the only thing he cared about.

It meant everything.

It was his entire world.

The only forever he desired.

# CHAPTER 2

Rook caught up with the angel just as he reached the plateau that overlooked the bottomless pit. The fortress rose beyond it, piercing the black vault of Hell, flickering golden light from the broad river of lava that snaked across the land below him illuminating it. A desire to reach that fortress and forget the intruder pounded inside him, tugged at his chest, but he ignored it.

The angel was his means of securing the position he desired.

His only desire.

He grinned as he closed in, beat his wings harder and narrowed the distance between them down to a few metres.

His crimson eyes briefly leaped beyond the male to sweep over the plateau, and his grin stretched wider. The angels of this male's ranks who normally called it home were nowhere to be seen.

The fool had no backup.

Did he honestly believe himself strong enough to take him on alone? Powerful enough to battle an entire legion of Hell's angels? Not just a legion, but *the* legion. The First Battalion. They had carved their name in bone and written it in blood. They were decimators, destroyers of any who stood in their way, an unstoppable force.

And he was their second in command.

The angel landed and jogged forwards a few steps, towards an outcrop of black rocks that rose near the right edge of the plateau, surrounding the pool.

Rook swept down and landed close behind him.

The male slowly turned and Rook scowled at him, his audacity grating on Rook's last nerve. Still the angel showed no fear. He strode towards the angel, filled with a need to beat it out of him, to punish him for daring to be so calm when he was achingly close to the Devil's fortress.

His master's voice curled around him, burrowing deep into him and filling him with strength. He tipped his chin up and called on his demonic form again. His bones lengthened, muscles bulging beneath his skin as it blackened, and he flashed his teeth as they sharpened and turned crimson.

"I almost recognised him for a moment there." The voice was male, and foreign, didn't issue from the angel before him.

He wasn't alone.

Rook snarled, refusing to let the fact the angel had a comrade dissuade him. He felt no fear. He felt only resolve, the deepest of desires. He had come to claim this angel as his prize, and he would continue with that mission. In fact, he would claim this angel's companion too.

The Devil was sure to be pleased.

The owner of the voice stepped out from behind the jagged mound of basalt and casually leaned a hip against it as he folded his arms across his broad chest. The tawny-haired male's rich brown eyes were sharp and focused as they assessed him.

Rook assessed him in return, not missing the fact he wore mortal clothing of a black shirt with the sleeves rolled up his corded forearms and black jeans paired with leather boots.

Definitely not missing the fact the male seemed to have lost something.

His wings.

A fallen angel.

"It's definitely Rook?" The brunet looked to the dark angel.

"Yes, Einar... I'm sure of it." The angel glanced over his shoulder at the one called Einar. "Although he claims he does not know any witches."

Einar's eyebrows rose. "Maybe they messed with his head."

Rook growled. "You're the ones trying to fuck with my head."

The brunet glanced at his companion. "He certainly sounds like the Rook we knew."

Rook refused to let his words sway him. Neither of them knew him. He had met the dark angel before in Hell and that was the only reason he felt familiar. He didn't know this fallen angel.

"Your trick is elaborate, I give you that." Rook walked to his left, slowly circling the two males, studying them and gathering all the information he could without engaging them. "Do you think bringing a fallen angel will sway me and make me believe you're not out to hurt me... or perhaps you think it will make me believe you're some sort of ally of my kind? I hate to disappoint, but it won't work."

"No one is out to fool you, Rook." The dark angel stepped forwards and the twin blades in his hands dematerialised. "And neither of us mean you harm."

He focused on the fallen one as he slowly edged around, closer to him. It was possible the male was concealing his wings, pretending to be fallen. As the dark angel moved out of his line of sight, clearing the path between him and Einar, the power the black-winged deceiver emanated grew weaker, enough that Rook got a clearer sense of Einar's power.

It was bound.

Rook had met fallen angels, most of them shortly before they pledged themselves to his master and became like him. This male had all the markers they had borne, a sense that whatever power they had once commanded, it was muted now, hidden beneath layers of pain that ran soul-deep.

"My battalion is coming." Rook's gaze darted between them, gauging their reaction to that news.

Neither seemed fazed.

He wanted to grin as it dawned on him that they weren't going to flee. They intended to fight. The fallen angel would be an easy target, and his pain-in-the-ass comrade would be distracted by protecting him when the battle happened. Capturing them both was going to be almost too easy. He could almost taste that promotion.

Before the metaphorical night was through, he would be one of only a handful of angels trusted by the Devil as his right-hand men.

From there, he would work his way up through that group, tearing down any who stood in his way.

Although, achieving the role of his master's closest advisor and most-trusted angel would be impossible.

It belonged to the brute, Asmodeus.

An angel who Rook had never seen, had only heard the bloody rumours about. He was legendary. A monster who terrified the demons that inhabited Hell, and one who even some of the Devil's angels feared.

"Take this." Einar's bass voice snapped him back to the foolish angels who were about to become his ticket to glory and power.

Rook scowled at the white card he offered, one that was barely the size of the male's palm.

Einar glanced at his comrade. "I don't think he's going to make this easy, Apollyon."

"It is a shame that Taylor refused to set foot in this realm. We could have used her help." The black-haired angel took the card from Einar, and questions about the female he had called Taylor fled as the male shifted his blue eyes to land on him.

Apollyon.

Rook knew this male's name.

It was almost as legendary as that of Asmodeus.

This angel was destined to battle the Devil at set intervals, his master's freedom hinging on whether he won or was defeated. Rumour had it that if he won, the Devil could walk free of Hell. Rook couldn't vouch for how true that was. He only knew tales of the Devil being defeated and confined within his fortress until the power that held him there weakened, allowing him to stray into the lands surrounding it.

"Just take a look." Apollyon turned the white card towards him.

Rook's eyes fell to it.

A strange sense of longing swept through him.

Confused the hell out of him.

He didn't know the ethereal female someone had sketched on the card.

Her pale eyes seemed to hold him though, as if she possessed some power over him, and he couldn't tear his away from her.

"This is Isadora," Apollyon said in a low voice, "and she needs your help. You were her guardian once."

The spell shattered.

His gaze snapped up to meet Apollyon's.

Instantly dropped back to her again as a thousand questions boiled inside him, twisted him in knots he tried to untangle and free himself from. Whenever he came close to convincing himself it was all a ruse, the threads of those questions tightened around him, holding him fast.

He stared at the female. *Isadora.*

Her name rang in the chaos of his mind.

"Isadora is the witch I told you about. The one who needs your help, Rook." Apollyon's tone was measured, each word spoken carefully, as if the male feared rousing him from his reverie.

It wasn't possible.

Nothing could stop him from looking at her.

Isadora. A witch. His ward?

He shook his head. "I've been an angel of Hell for centuries... no witch can live that long. They're as mortal as the humans. You're lying to me."

Yet he still couldn't tear his gaze away from her.

"We don't know how she has survived so long," Einar said and he sensed the male move away from the rocks, coming to stand beside Apollyon.

"We only know that she is in danger, Rook." Apollyon.

That same collected tone, each word spoken in a way that irked Rook for some reason. Always with the damned control. For once, Rook wanted to see him let loose. He wanted to see him raise hell.

Why?

The desire winked out of existence before Rook could find the answer to that question. It meant nothing. He focused on the drawing of the female. Isadora. Was she something?

She was nothing.

He felt he should feel that, but it didn't stick. The sensation she stirred in him remained, setting him on edge, making him restless with a need to do something.

Fight the angels and claim his position as one of the Devil's trusted men?

Or save her?

"We need to find her." Apollyon moved the picture closer to him. "The people who have her might be hurting her right now."

He growled, the violence of it shocking him together with the urge that bolted through him, lit up his blood and had him stretching his leathery wings—he needed to find her. The thought of her coming to harm had his fangs lengthening, his lips peeling back off them as he gripped his blade.

He needed to save her.

He shook his head, staggered back a step, and wrenched his gaze away from her picture. It was a lie. A trick.

"You have to believe us, Rook." Einar stepped towards him but Apollyon held his arm out at his side, blocking the male's path to him.

Rook growled and snapped his fangs at them as he burrowed the fingers of his free hand through his thick black hair. He gripped his skull so hard that it hurt, squeezing it tightly. It was better than the pain of the thoughts spinning through his mind, ones that had him unsure whether he was coming or going, confused about everything as twin needs warred inside him.

Capture the angels and secure his position.

Or save her?

He stumbled back another step.

His master's voice reached him through the clamour of his thoughts, luring his eyes away from the deceivers to the fortress beyond them.

The First Battalion filled the sky between him and the castle.

His men were coming.

Relief swept through him, threatening to rip his strength from him. He pushed the weakness aside and readied his blade, resolve flooding him as he turned back towards the angels.

They looked over their shoulders.

"Time to leave." Einar grabbed Apollyon's arm and the dark angel glared at him. "If we're dead, we can't help her."

No. Rook wasn't going to let them escape.

He launched at them on a snarl.

Apollyon turned his glare on him and power pressed down on Rook, slowing his movements as it buffeted him, had his muscles growing sluggish as his body fought against the strength of it. He growled and kept pressing forwards, each step harder than the last. The bastard was stronger than Rook had suspected, commanded power far beyond any angel he had met before.

But he wasn't going to let that stop him.

He just had to delay the male long enough for his legion to reach them.

Apollyon spread his huge black wings, grabbed Einar around his waist and lifted into the air with a single powerful beat.

Rook unleashed a roar and lumbered towards them, intent on stopping them from getting away.

The dark angel was over twenty metres above him by the time he mustered enough of his own power to push back against the overwhelming force of Apollyon's. The second he was sure his wings wouldn't fail him, Rook beat them and kicked upwards, propelling himself towards the angel.

Apollyon glanced down, his face dark as the black slashes of his eyebrows knitted hard above his blue eyes.

"Think about it, Rook," the male bit out and grimaced as he flew harder, increasing the distance between them. "Really think about her."

He cast his free hand towards Rook and the white card whirled out of his grip, twirled and pirouetted as it danced down towards him. Another wave of power hit him so hard he was knocked from the air. He plummeted to the ground, passing the picture and disturbing its flight.

He grunted as he slammed into the black basalt, his knees taking the brunt of the blow, sending pain ricocheting up his femurs and spine. The sketch of the female swirled into view and gently came to rest before him.

Really think about her?

He reached out and plucked it from the ground, lifted it and stared hard at her face, that odd feeling lingering inside him. He canted his head to his left. Did he know her?

He had never seen her before.

The sensation of Apollyon's power faded as another rose to replace it.

That of his master.

He swiftly pushed onto his feet and found himself slipping the picture of the witch into the waist of his armour as he twisted to face the fortress.

At the edge of the plateau, the toes of his polished black Italian leather shoes barely touching the flat slab of rock, stood his master.

The Devil.

The black-haired male adjusted the cuffs of the obsidian shirt he wore beneath his tailored black suit jacket, an air of irritation about him as his crimson eyes tracked the two intruders. Something crossed those eyes as the portal opened, a vast crack in the vault of Hell.

Rook looked up, glimpsing blue beyond all the blackness.

The mortal world.

He dropped his gaze back to his master, and the brief longing that had lit his eyes was gone, replaced with pure darkness as they narrowed.

"What did they want?" The Devil lowered his eyes to Rook, his deep voice deceptively mellow.

"I believe they meant to use the pool." He wasn't sure why he lied, but fuck, it unsettled him, had him twitchy as he shifted back, letting his demonic form fall away. "One of them was fallen."

"A fallen angel in Hell that doesn't belong to me?" The Devil arched his left eyebrow. "And what made you interfere?"

Rook hiked his shoulders. "I thought to capture them."

The truth.

"Alone?" The Devil's eyebrow lifted higher and the crimson in his eyes faded, revealing the gold of his irises.

He couldn't risk lying any more to his master, needed to find a way to deflect the male's questions away from what the angel and the fallen one had wanted. He liked his head where it was, on his shoulders, and the position of it was likely to change if the Devil discovered he had lied.

At the very least, it would screw up his chances of achieving command of the First Battalion.

That legion of Hell's angels hovered in the air behind his master.

"No." Rook jerked his chin towards his men. "They were late."

"And were not dispatched by you when you first encountered the maggot. I had to dispatch them. Why?" Shadows flitted across the Devil's sculpted features and Rook braced himself.

His master was known for his mercurial temperament.

He wouldn't get any warning if the Devil decided to take his head. Maybe that was a good thing. He wasn't sure he wanted to know in advance if he was going to die and end up serving Heaven again, stripped of all his memories to start anew as an angel.

Had he been a guardian angel as Apollyon and Einar believed?

Had the witch been his ward?

He pushed those questions aside. "The angel thought to taunt me. It distracted me. You summoned them before I could."

"A trait very unlike him. Apollyon does not taunt. So what was the real reason he came to you?" The Devil looked as if he wanted to close the distance between them and a flare of crimson ringed his pupils when he looked down at his feet.

The power that kept him confined was fading, but evidently his master couldn't move further from his fortress than his current position.

Not wanting to enrage the one he served, Rook obediently moved towards him, showing the Devil that he didn't intend to remain beyond his reach. He did not fear his master, was his to command, and he trusted the male.

He stopped when he was within reach of the Devil, bowed his head and pressed his left hand to the chest of his crimson-edged black breastplate. "He attempted to make me believe I know him. When I resisted and mentioned the legion had been dispatched, he fled to this plateau where I pursued him and he revealed a fallen angel was with him. I believe he intended to fool me into following them from this realm by making himself appear an ally of the male... one who is like me."

"You are powerful, Rook. There are those in this world who would like you removed from my company." The Devil lifted his left hand, smoothed his palm along the straight line of Rook's jaw, and viciously closed his fingers around his throat. He forced Rook's head up so their eyes met. "But are you sure that is the only reason they were here?"

Rook managed a nod.

The Devil's grip on him tightened, short black claws pressing into his flesh, and he choked as he fought for air.

His master smiled coldly. "I would hate for you to lie to me, my dearest Rook."

"No lie," he ground out as he struggled to breathe. "I wanted to... capture them... to please you... all I wanted."

The Devil's gold-to-crimson eyes brightened as his smile gained warmth and he released Rook's neck to pat his cheek.

"You have always pleased me." He turned away from Rook, all of the warmth leaving his voice as he added, "make sure it continues to be that way."

He disappeared.

Rook waited for the legion to leave before he let his legs give out, landed on his knees on the plateau and stared at the fortress.

Why hadn't he told his master about the female?

It had been on the tip of his tongue, at the front of his mind to do so, but something had stopped him. He pressed a hand to his bare stomach. It swirled and swayed, uneasy as he considered telling the Devil about the witch.

Rook pushed onto his feet, a need to be alone rushing through him. He kicked off and spread his wings, swiftly covered the distance between him and his basic quarters in the camp belonging to the First Battalion. He ignored the questions of his men as he landed, strode through the busy camp and ducked through the open door of the black stone building that was his home.

He shut the wooden door behind him and slumped onto the flat slab that served as his sole piece of furniture.

Why had the thought of telling his master about Isadora given him a bad feeling, one that lingered even now?

Why couldn't he bring himself to tell the Devil everything? His master was just that—the one who commanded him, deserved his absolute and unwavering loyalty.

But he had lied to him today.

More than once.

And he hadn't done it to keep his head on his shoulders or ensure he could still achieve the position he desired.

He had done it to protect the witch.

He looked around, checking no one was outside the open spaces in the walls that acted as windows in his small hut, and focused his senses to make sure everyone was at a distance.

Satisfied he would be undisturbed, he leaned to one side and carefully pulled the white card from the waist of his armour. He settled it in his palm and hunched over, resting his elbows on his knees as he stared at it.

Stared at her.

Isadora.

Why had he hidden her from the Devil?

Apollyon and Einar were wrong. He didn't know her.

She was beautiful though, bore no resemblance to the human females he had met in the past. There was an otherworldliness to her, something about her making her appear more fantasy than reality. He shook his head at that. She was a drawing, and for all he knew, she wasn't even real. She could be another lie, told to him by the angel to make him falter and tempt him away from Hell.

Whoever had drawn her had done well though, evoking an image that was mysterious and enticing, and strong yet delicate. Delicate? She was a witch. Witches were powerful, dangerous, and known to be vicious, ruthless in their pursuit of power.

He didn't remember ever meeting one, but once or twice in his lifetime, he had visited places where there had been some. Whenever he had discovered witches were present, he'd had an odd urge to avoid them. Something about them made him wary, had him wanting to keep his distance and ensure they didn't see him.

He wasn't sure why.

Had a witch done something terrible to him in a past life?

Had it been her?

Rook scrubbed his eyes and shoved the sketch under the pillow that rested at the end of the bench furthest from the door. She was a lie. A fabrication. He had to forget about her.

He considered burning her picture by tossing it into one of the arteries of lava that criss-crossed the valley not far from him.

For some reason, the thought of destroying it caused a tight knot in his breast.

He settled on ignoring it instead and focusing on resting, because he had patrols to lead later and an interrogation to oversee at the prison. He didn't need the angels or the witch distracting him. If they wanted to save her, they would find a way. There was no reason for him to get involved.

Rook unbuckled his greaves and removed his boots, and then stripped off his vambraces, placing them close to the head of his bench in case he needed them. He could easily manifest them on his body rather than manually donning them, but he was tired, in need of rest, and wanted to conserve his strength. He rolled his shoulders and reached for the buckle on the right side of his breastplate, tilting his head downwards at the same time.

He froze.

Stared at the four-inch band of ink that wrapped around his forearm just above his wrist.

His eyes charted the intricate black and violet swirls, picking out the hints of blue and red that hid among the design. He'd had them for as long as he could remember, but he didn't recall where or when he had got them done. They were beautiful though, captivated him whenever he looked at them, and the more he stared at them, the stronger a feeling inside him grew.

They meant something.

He had studied tattoos in his free time, had visited establishments that specialised in them in the mortal world, but no one had been able to tell him what they meant. Some settlements in Hell had males of his kind who were dedicated to inking their brethren with designs related to both Earth and this realm.

Whenever he considered approaching them to ask about his own ink, a chill swept through him and he found himself covering the designs with his vambraces again, keeping them hidden.

He wasn't sure where that feeling came from. He just knew it was important that none of his kind knew about them.

It was important no one saw them.

He forced his wings away, twisted at the waist and lay back on the solid stone slab. He sighed as he rested his head on the pillow and pressed his right foot against the far wall of his cramped quarters, and bent his left leg at the knee.

He studied the swirls within the matching bands that circled his forearms and let himself get lost in them.

What did they mean?

Why did he feel it was important that no one saw them?

He wanted answers, but he would find none in Hell. Would he find them in the mortal realm if he ventured there again?

An urge to leave Hell and fly in the azure sky of the human world surged through him, one he felt sure stemmed not from a need to know what his ink meant but from something else.

He pulled the picture of the female from beneath his pillow and lifted it, held it above him and frowned at it.

Did he know her?

He didn't think so, but as he looked at her, a feeling hit him, one that was powerful and commanding.

He wanted to know her.

He wanted to leave Hell and search for her.

He needed to see if he *could* find her.

Because if he could, then she might be able to answer all the questions that plagued him. She might be the key.

One that would unlock a past he couldn't remember.

# CHAPTER 3

Isadora had been a damned fool.

She clenched her teeth together as the vehicle bounced and swayed, rumbling along what felt like a track rather than a road now. She flexed her fingers in her lap, cursing the heavy cuffs that weighed her wrists down.

Manacles that had her drowsy, weak with a lack of power as they suppressed it, stealing it from her.

Spells weren't the only things they were using against her.

She blinked hard behind the hood that covered her head and struggled to focus through the haze of the drugs as they finally began to leave her system.

The bastards had started drugging her whenever they moved her after the first long drive, where she had revealed that the spell on the shackles wasn't enough to completely bind her magic. She could perform low-level spells if she really concentrated and was given enough time to gather the strength to cast them.

Her first failed attempt at escape had ended with her knocked out cold by one of the men in the group.

After that, they had been more cautious, using spells to keep her compliant whenever they were questioning her and drugs to keep her weakened when they were on the move.

Apparently, losing her wasn't an option. She was their 'payday'. Isadora gritted her teeth at that, anger blazing through her blood to burn away the chill of the drug. She wasn't a damned payday. She was a living, breathing being.

Well, she was breathing anyway.

She wasn't sure she had been living for a long time now.

Drifting perhaps.

Existing.

She lowered her head and exhaled, blowing the black material away from her mouth, and fought the pain that surged within her. It was endless and deep, always ready to grip her whenever her strength faltered.

It faltered a lot these days.

Days that were too long, stretched minutes into hours and seemed as infinite as her pain.

She lifted her hands, needing to rub at the sore spot between her breasts, where she ached the fiercest.

The man beside her grunted something. He grabbed her arm, shoved her hands back into her lap with enough force that her wrists hurt as they smashed against the metal of her shackles.

Mother Earth, she had been a fool.

She had believed in someone again.

They had betrayed her, had hit her with a spell that had stripped her power from her and had left her defenceless.

She curled forwards. The man pulled her back, slamming her spine into the side of the van.

"Something's wrong with her," he hollered, his French accent thick.

A regal British male voice answered from her right, in the vehicle's cab. "Hit her with another dose then. It's still a few miles."

She had named him Country Estate. She had given each of the five a name, had been slowly learning about them, devouring every drop of information they gave her whenever they slipped up, and even when they didn't. Country Estate was second in command, and both the man beside her, Frenchie, and the one driving the vehicle, London Town, deferred to him. The other male in the group, Spanish Inquisition, only took orders from the group's leader, a brunette who Isadora had named Bitch.

"We're all out," Frenchie answered.

"There's more where we're heading. Hit her with a spell instead."

*Witches.*

She sneered that word in her head.

Sometimes, her kind could be worse than the demons. Worse than the Devil himself.

She erased that thought, because no one was worse than the Devil. Whatever these men did, it would never compare to what that dark fiend had done to her. He had taken everything from her.

He had stolen her forever.

And it had been all her fault.

She curled forwards again, the pain too much to bear as memories surfaced to torment her, to strip her strength from her as surely as the spell Frenchie muttered. A spell he didn't need.

It washed over her anyway, mercifully stealing away some of that pain. Her mind grew hazier, thoughts swirling together until they made no sense and peace swept through her, a sweet oblivion that gave her relief.

She jostled in time with the van and Frenchie, rocked and swayed and didn't care as heat stole through her, the spell binding her powers and leaving her weak again.

Weak enough to finally die?

She craved death.

Needed it more than answers most days, and some of those days she had even attempted it. It never stuck. She had learned early on that attempting to die was a recipe for a long and painful recovery.

While she was deathless, immortal now in a way, she wasn't invulnerable. She was still mortal. Her bones took weeks to mend, still caused her pain when the weather was against her.

Her right shin and left wrist ached right now, a response to the cold of the van that smelled of snow.

How long had these witches had her under lock and key?

This morning, she had thought it had been weeks, but as she breathed deep of the tinny air, she realised it had to be months. Winter was here.

How far had they moved her from Paris?

She had been an idiot to head there, drawn by the rumours an angel had been spotted in the city, one bearing black wings.

She had been hopeful for the first time in centuries though and the thought it might be an angel she had once known, one who might know her still, had been too alluring to resist. She had gone to the city, had asked around among the witches, desperate to meet him because she had hoped he could lift some of the shadows from her heart.

She had hoped he could tell her how the angel she had loved and lost was.

And maybe part of her had hoped that she could see that angel again.

Rook.

Her desperation had led her into a trap.

This group of witches had told her they had seen an angel and knew where to find him. She had gone with them to a grand building in the suburbs of the city, had foolishly followed them inside, led by the hope they could give her answers she had badly needed for over a thousand years.

In the foyer of that building, Bitch had been waiting with her ice-blond bodyguard, Spanish Inquisition. The man had watched her through glacial grey eyes as she had approached the regal brunette, his gaze calculating, and when she had been within a few metres, he had told her to stop.

When she had asked them for the information they had promised her, Bitch had told her they had heard rumours too.

Ones about her.

They had heard a witch with silver hair and aquamarine eyes didn't age.

Couldn't die.

She chuckled mirthlessly beneath her breath at that, earning a sharp strike across the side of her head from her guard. She toppled to her right, her shoulder slamming into the bench, and lay there, staring into the darkness, feeling nothing but that twisted sense of déjà vu over what had happened.

Once upon a time, someone else had told her she would have something and then a dark prince had stolen everything from her instead.

A monster she never wanted to meet again.

These fools thought she could give them the secret to eternal life. Another chuckle escaped her. It wasn't going to happen.

She focused on her wrists where they rested in front of her, dangling off the edge of the bench. The secret was hidden beneath her shackles and layers of spells, concealed from even her own eyes.

It was ancient and forgotten by the world, and she was going to keep it that way.

She wouldn't let these people know it, no matter what they did to her.

If they got hold of it, they would use it to force an immortal being into a bond with them, believing it would make them more powerful.

It had happened in the past.

When she had been researching the spell, she had learned of witches who had bound immortals to them through force. Most of the stories ended with either the witch being murdered on repeat by the immortal to punish them or the immortal managing to kill themselves in order to escape being a slave.

When she had gotten her hands on the manuscript containing the spell, she had destroyed it after using it. She could remember it though, knew the words she needed to say and the ingredients required to cast it.

While she wished pain upon the witches who had her, she wasn't cruel enough to give them the spell in order to watch them suffer at the hands of an immortal. She wasn't vicious enough to inflict that torment, that slavery, upon an innocent immortal.

Revenge wasn't her style. Her family had never been one for it.

Were they still that way?

Her bloodline had practiced tolerance, learning to live in a world doing good rather than evil.

If she had a chance for revenge against the ones who had taken everything from her, was assured she would be the victor and not captured and tortured for eternity, would she take it?

Mother Earth, she might.

She was tired now, worn down to nothing. If there was a chance she could have some closure, she would seize it. It would be worth coping with whatever bones broke or organs ruptured during the battle, because it would ease at least a little of her pain.

Her heart would feel lighter knowing the one who had orchestrated her suffering had paid the price.

The vehicle squeaked to a stop.

A chill breeze blasted against her as the back doors opened, the scent of snow growing stronger as air swept into the van.

Frenchie grabbed her arm and tugged her upright. She stumbled along behind him, trying to focus on her surroundings in the darkness so she didn't fall. She had done that once and they had struck her so hard that her cheekbone had fractured.

It was no longer healing, which backed up the feeling she had been their captive for months now.

"Where'd you get this gaff?" It was the other British male, the one whose more cockney than country estate accent had earned him the moniker of London Town.

They were cautious, hadn't used names around her the entire time they had been holding her.

Afraid she might get revenge on them by using their names?

Names were powerful. They allowed the more potent spells to take hold, and some of them required a name as part of the incantation. Without one, she couldn't use such a spell. With one, she could easily curse them to suffer greatly. Horrifically.

She was feeling imaginative recently too. If they slipped up and gave her their names, she might be inclined to curse them into lusting after each other.

She stifled a smile as Frenchie marched her through snow that bit into her feet through her thin leather boots and soaked into her black jeans, not feeling the cold as her mind wandered pleasant paths, following thoughts of cursing them.

With their staunch masculinity, she could well imagine how horrified they would be if they were unable to keep their hands off each other. It would certainly be entertaining.

Maybe she would even curse them to hunger after every male they came across, make them unable to resist the need to flirt with every one of them, even if those men threatened them.

She stumbled a little as her boots hit gravel.

Frenchie pulled her up again, muttering, "Let's just get inside. I'm freezing my balls off."

"Take our guest to the basement. My sister called ahead to have the staff get everything ready." Country Estate moved away from them at a swifter clip, his expensive fragrance fading as the distance between them grew.

"Reckon they own this gaff too?" London Town sidled closer, until his cheap cologne overpowered her, choking her.

It was difficult enough to breathe with the hood on. She didn't need him suffocating her with his stench.

While she despised them all, London Town and Frenchie could learn a few things from Country Estate. Personal hygiene being one of them.

Frenchie didn't answer. Isadora imagined him glaring at London Town in a pointed way, one that warned the man to be more careful because he had just given her the first real piece of information they had offered in the entire time she had been their captive.

Country Estate and Bitch's accents weren't just for show, and neither were their refined air and high-and-mighty attitudes. They had money, apparently enough to own this new location and one of the previous ones. Which one? Paris or one of the handful that had come afterwards?

More than one of them?

There were only a few dozen witch bloodlines in England with money to their name. If she did a little research, it wouldn't be difficult to narrow it down to the one they belonged to, or possibly led.

Another vehicle pulled up, growling as it crunched over the snow and onto the gravel, and her guard paused, turning slightly towards the sound.

Low voices sounded, Bitch and her bodyguard, and Isadora strained to hear what they were talking about as they closed the doors of the sports car.

They always travelled separately. She had noticed that when they had moved her the first time. She had noticed several other things since then.

Like the fact the brunette and Spanish Inquisition were an item but they were keeping it secret from the others for some reason. Because Country Estate wouldn't approve of his big sister sleeping with one of the group? Or because the group might feel he was being given preferential treatment, was sleeping his way to the top and liable to get more out of their shady business because of it?

During the times they had been sent to interrogate or guard her, Frenchie and London Town had complained about the fact Bitch was keeping things from them. They didn't like the fact she went to meetings with other witches and never told them what had happened, or why she had been meeting with them in the first place.

Was Bitch thinking of selling the spell once she got her hands on it?

Many witches in the world would pay handsomely for such a lost incantation, one that held the power to make them immortal.

The scent of Country Estate grew stronger again, and she heard him mutter, "Bloody cold here as always."

He had never been cruel to her, had been patient the times he had been sent to get the spell out of her.

In fact, only one of them had really hurt her.

It was the reason she had called him Spanish Inquisition.

He never asked her questions when he was sent to her, never attempted to get the spell out of her through means other than his fists. For a powerful witch, he certainly liked attacking physically. He would spend an hour with her hurting her in silence, that coldness in his grey eyes, as if he took no pleasure from what he was doing. She knew he savoured every blow that made her cry out, relished bending her limbs until they felt as if they would break and she screamed for him to stop. The bastard was sadistic, vicious.

He almost made the Devil look like a sweetheart.

Almost.

Spanish Inquisition always stopped at the critical moment, before bone broke or flesh split. The Devil hadn't. He had torn her apart and then had one of his angels heal her so he could do it all over again.

"I have a meeting in the south, but I should be back within a few days." Bitch's voice was loud, just off to Isadora's right, and she turned her head in that direction and focused there, trying to use a low-level spell to sense where she was.

She didn't have the strength to cast one though, not when the spell Frenchie had used on her was still flowing through her together with the lingering effects of the drug. She resigned herself to listening.

"A meeting?" Country Estate didn't sound happy. "When did this come up?"

"They called during the drive." Spanish Inquisition's deep voice cut like a diamond in the still night air, brooking no argument from Country Estate. "I will go with her to make sure she's safe."

Isadora bet he would be doing a lot more than keeping her safe. He would be keeping her satisfied too. She didn't want to imagine what sort of twisted play happened in their bedchamber. She barely suppressed a shudder.

"It's important." Bitch again, with the same amount of bite as Spanish Inquisition. "I leave you in charge, Brother. I expect results when I return. I want that spell."

The sound of footsteps drifted away from Isadora and then the purr of the sports car's engine filled the tense silence.

"*Results*," Country Estate sneered and then barked, "Get her in the fucking house."

Frenchie yanked on her upper arm and she stumbled as she violently twisted on her heel, struggled to keep her balance as he marched her towards the building.

"Step up." Frenchie lifted her arm.

Isadora blindly raised her right foot, snagged it on the lip of the step, and fell forwards. He yanked her up again with a huff.

"Perhaps if I wasn't blindfolded, I would be less of a burden," she snapped.

"She's lucid." London Town.

Dammit.

She hadn't meant to give away the fact she had managed to shake off the spell back in the van. It was growing less effective the more they used it on her, her magic learning to counter it even when it was mostly bound by the spell on the shackles. They were going to resort to drugs again, and she didn't have a counter against those, despised the way they made her feel, stealing away sensation and her awareness with it, leaving her vulnerable.

As much as she craved oblivion, she didn't like it.

Warmth washed over her, together with the scent of a log fire, and light penetrated the hood over her head. Frenchie marched her forwards, into darkness again, down a stone staircase. She focused on her surroundings, reached out with what little magic she had at her disposal to form a picture of her new location.

A rush of sensation flooded her as she connected with magic that gave her subdued abilities a boost. Nature. That magic formed a key element of hers, was the basis of most of her spells and her power. The light.

She used the sudden boost in her magic to map the area before Frenchie or anyone else noticed she was siphoning power from everything beyond the walls of the building.

A building that was old.

Easily several centuries.

It was embedded in the landscape now, the magic twined around it, burrowed deeply into the fabric of it.

It had been a long time since she had felt power like this.

The magic was dormant and powerful. Not power a witch like Country Estate and his companions could tap into. They probably weren't even aware of it. Users of the dark rarely felt the touch of the light. It was beautiful, potent, and stirred her strength. It flowed around her, woven into the trees that spread out in all directions around her and the mountains beyond them.

A forest and mountains she wanted to see, sure they would bring her some relief because her own magic was in tune with the light, threaded through and entwined with that of nature. Magic meant to give, not take. Create and not destroy.

Frenchie pushed her forwards and she staggered, boots scuffing against stone as she fought to remain upright. She flinched as he whipped the hood off, turning her face away from him and the sudden brightness that assaulted her eyes.

He chuckled.

"Enjoy your new home." His pale blue eyes matched hers as they leaped to meet his, but his were glacial, held no feeling as he gazed at her, and no remorse as he raked them down her body. "We'll have to see about getting you cleaned up. You're starting to tarnish."

She glared at him through the tangled threads of her silver hair and spat, "I'm not an object."

A smile tilted his lips, tugging at the left corner of his wide mouth, and he hiked his broad shoulders, raising his long black coat with them. "Could've fooled me."

He turned away and her chest tightened as she realised he was heading towards a thick steel door, one that looked like a new addition to the stone room.

A cell.

They had placed her in a cell.

Panic closed her throat and she launched for the exit.

Slammed into the cold metal door as it shut in her face.

Her shackles scraped against it as she pressed her hands to it, searching for the handle, and cold slithered through her as she realised something. There wasn't one.

"Make yourself comfortable, Isadora. We're going to be here until you finally give up."

With that, he walked away, his boots loud on the stone floor.

A floor she wanted to sink to as her strength left her, despair eating away at it until there was nothing left. They had never placed her in a cell before, had always held her in a room, where she had some comforts. Now she was in a bare stone box, cold and alone in the dark. She forced herself to remain standing, refused to give up and give in to them. She wouldn't give them the secret they wanted from her. It was hers to keep and she *would* take it to her grave.

If her grave would welcome her.

If death could be hers.

She looked around at the dark cell, a bare room that extended no more than fifteen feet in all directions, and leaned back against the door. It was cold against her back, chilled her skin through her thin black t-shirt. She hated her clothes, not because of their style but because Country Estate had given them to her in an attempt to win her over when Spanish Inquisition had torn her own clothes from her in an attempt of a different nature—one meant to break her.

She wouldn't break.

She couldn't.

She lifted her blue gaze and fixed it on the long rectangular window set high into the wall opposite her. Bars lined the wide opening, glass shielding her from the weather on the other side. Even without the bars, she wouldn't be able to escape that way. The height of the window was too small, barely six inches. She would never be able to squeeze through a gap like that.

Isadora drifted towards it anyway, drawn by the sliver of moonlight shining through it.

Snow edged the lower part of the window and as she tiptoed and gripped the bars to pull herself up so she could get a better view of the world outside, she hoped it wouldn't rise any higher.

Beyond the white garden that extended at eye level to her, breathtaking mountains speared the sky, the snow that covered them shining bright blue in the cold moonlight. Mottled darkness spread over their bases, signalling the trees she had felt.

She had never been given a view before, and while she found it comforting, it also set her on edge.

Because it meant they were so far from civilisation they didn't fear her recognising where they were or getting help from anyone.

Where was she?

Wherever it was, it was a long way from Paris. There were no mountains in that region of France. Bitch had mentioned going south. If Isadora had to guess, she would place them near the border with Switzerland, perhaps far enough south that Bitch was travelling to Nice.

Why did they keep moving her?

Was it because they were meeting with buyers for the spell? Or did they fear the angel she had been seeking would come after her? As far as she knew, he wasn't aware of her. They had no reason to fear him.

They were definitely the group she had heard about during her time in Paris. Rumour had it they had been stealing magic from witches and using it to give them more power, but Isadora now suspected they were also selling the spells they extracted.

Was that the reason they kept moving? To sell spells and evade those who might come after them? She was sure other witches were trying to hunt them down, desperate to save their loved ones or have revenge on the ones who had taken them.

She rubbed her shackled wrist, feeling a glimmer of the magic hidden there.

It had been a blessing once, but now it felt like a curse. She was damned to walk the Earth, aware that Rook was back in Heaven and no longer remembered her. The spell was proof of that. He was alive because it was still active, linking them.

She twisted, pressed her back to the stone wall and slid down it to land on her backside on the cold floor.

She stroked her fingers across her left wrist and focused, aching to see through the layers of the spell to the markings they concealed. She needed the comfort of them as everything took its toll on her. She needed hope again.

Faint swirls shimmered on her skin and tears filled her eyes at the sight of them.

Grief swept through her, as strong now as it had been on the day he had been taken from her. She mourned for all she had lost and would never know again.

Rook had forgotten her, but she would never forget him.

Her guardian angel.

She traced the swirls she could see above her heavy manacles, stared at them and sank into despair even as she tried to remain strong. Some days, she wished the spell had been temporary, one designed to end with the true death of one of them.

Other days, she loved that it wasn't.

She loved that it was eternal and unbreakable.

Because it was what Rook had wanted.

But now he was gone, and she was alone in this world, cursed to an eternity without him.

Now she ached for death.

The hope she had of seeing him again had been worn down to nothing but a tiny seed now, one she foolishly nurtured from time to time even when she knew it would only hurt her. It was better to let go of any hope of meeting him again. Even if she did meet him, it wouldn't give her relief. Not when he wouldn't remember her.

She let the markings fade, watched the spells fall back into place to hide them from her. They were still there though. She could feel them. Warm against her skin. She sniffed back her tears, sucked down a breath and blew it out, trying to focus on happier times.

She had to be strong. She couldn't give up.

She knew more about her captors now. She just needed to keep working on them, getting them to lower their guards and slip up, revealing more about themselves.

She needed their names.

When she had them, she would destroy them.

She would save herself.

Because no one was coming to rescue her this time.

The sound of wings beating broke the frigid silence.

# CHAPTER 4

Rook flew low over the enormous prison, rolling left and right to avoid the jagged spires of black that rose from the sprawling high-walled building to form towers where the more rowdy and uncooperative of his master's captives were held.

He scanned the courtyard and the cells on the ravine side of the main building where one wall was missing, leaving the prisoners with the choice of attempting to escape.

The Devil did enjoy seeing how many of his captives would risk falling into the river of lava that snaked around the prison, seduced by the thought of being free.

So far, no one had made it out alive that way.

Maybe he should bring his master here. He was sure it would lift his mood. The Devil had been twitchy again today, more mercurial than usual. He had called Rook in for another round of questioning, going over his encounter with Apollyon and Einar all over again. Was his master expecting him to slip up?

It wasn't going to happen.

The Devil had given him good reason to keep the story he had told him in his report straight and not screw it up when he had arrived shortly after being summoned.

And had found his master in the fortress's courtyard, stood at the top of the broad black steps that led up to the immense doors of the building with both hands covered in blood.

Rook had looked at the bottom of the steps to find three glowing circles on the obsidian slabs.

All that was left of the three angels who had apparently displeased his master and had been returned to Heaven through death at his hands.

Not the end Rook desired for himself, so when he had been questioned in the very spot the males had died, he had spewed the same lies he had on the plateau.

He wasn't sure his master had bought them. Each time he was summoned, the Devil looked less like he believed him, and more strained. Why? What was plaguing him?

Rook wasn't the only one who had noticed the Devil was more over the edge than on it these days.

He could count at least a dozen reports of his master sending angels serving him back to Heaven in the signature bright white flashes of light. Hell, he had been on patrol yesterday and had witnessed what had looked like a damned lightning storm near the prison. The Devil must have killed at least thirty of his own men in the span of a few minutes.

No one was sure why.

It wasn't as if he could stroll up and ask what had him so cranky and quick to kill his own men.

Not without joining their ranks anyway.

The First Commander hoped that Asmodeus could talk their master down. Apparently, the brute had frequently been seen at the fortress over the past few days, since the angel incursion.

Asmodeus had come up with a solution, a way of soothing the Devil's fury.

The number of angel fatalities was decreasing each day, so the monster had to be doing something right. Rook hoped that was a good sign, because he was tiring of the duty that had been assigned to his squadron.

He swept down and dropped his feet, beat his broad crimson wings as he landed silently outside the prison.

"Are we sure it's enough?" Rook looked over today's offering.

Four scantily dressed mortal females huddled together on the black ground in front of his commander. A smattering of demons had been gathered too. Their sickly yellow gazes darted around as they stood off to one side, grouped so close together their dark scales blended to make them look like one demon with a hundred eyes.

"I hope so." His commander cast his grey gaze over the females in particular. "The men brought back an assortment today. They should appease one appetite while the demons will satisfy the other."

Rook hoped the Devil knew what to do with which. It seemed a shame to kill perfectly good females and disturbing to bed the demons.

"Take them." His commander signalled to the men guarding the humans and they nodded, grabbed a shrieking female each, and took flight.

Four more angels prodded the group of demons with their spears, forcing them to move.

"I'm going to take another look around and then head back to camp." Rook spread his wings.

His commander didn't take his eyes off the demons that were being led away. "I need you back within the hour. The Devil wants us to deal with some demons in the northern mountains, and you need to rest."

Rook nodded, kicked off and beat his wings, lifting into the air. He didn't want to rest. He needed to keep active or he ended up in his quarters, staring at the drawing of the witch.

Isadora.

If he could sleep and dream, he was sure she would be waiting there to torment him.

A feeling swirled inside him, pulling his focus to his left, away from the prison.

Speaking of torment.

The damned angel was back.

Rook drew the crimson sword from the sheath hanging at his waist, twisted and shot towards the plateau. He was done with Apollyon. He wouldn't allow the male to keep entering Hell, a place where he didn't belong, and certainly wouldn't allow him to make another attempt to sway him. He was sure it was the angel's presence and what he had tried to do that had the Devil in a foul mood.

He growled through his sharpening teeth as he closed in on the plateau and spotted the black-winged angel.

Apollyon hovered just feet above the flat slab of basalt, the glow of the rivers glinting off the gilded edges of his onyx armour.

Rook felt it when his focus shifted to him, the oppressive weight of the male's power bearing down on him, and snarled as he beat his wings harder, flew faster towards him, determined to end him.

The male stared him down but made no move to draw his weapons. He remained hovering in the air, an easy target.

On a wicked roar, Rook swept his hand along the length of his crimson blade, transforming it into a broadsword. He gripped it in both hands above his head and swung hard the moment he was within reach, aiming for Apollyon's left wing.

The male dodged right, narrowly evading the blow, and Rook growled as he followed through, the force of the swing dragging him down as the angel flew upwards.

Towards the portal.

His gaze snapped to it and he glimpsed a faint blue streak in the middle of the long crevasse in the dark ceiling of Hell.

Apollyon shot towards it, wings beating furiously.

No. He wasn't going to get away this time. Rook flapped his own wings and pursued him. Wind buffeted him as he manoeuvred beneath Apollyon and he swayed to his right, out of the vortex created by the angel's wings. The male glanced over his shoulder at him and flew harder in response, spiralled back into his path and tore a growl from Rook. He was trying to slow him down.

It wasn't going to happen.

He flew harder, faster, spun in the air and banked left as he put a burst of effort into his strokes, determined to capture Apollyon. Nothing would stop him this time. He grunted and flew harder still, ignoring the burn in his wings as he furiously pumped them. He almost drew level with the angel.

Apollyon cast him a black look and then strafed towards him, forcing Rook to drop to avoid a collision between their wings, losing the ground he had gained.

Son of a bitch.

He redoubled his effort to close the distance again, was so focused on drawing level with the bastard that he didn't notice breaking free of Hell.

It was only when a weight bloomed in his chest, tugging him downwards, that it dawned on him.

He turned in the air, driven to obey the command that pulled at him for an instant before it disappeared, and reached for the fracture in the pavement. The portal closed before he could reach it and he landed hard, pivoted on his heel and came to face Apollyon.

The male casually set down and furled his black wings against his back, his blue eyes cautious as he studied Rook.

"Open it again." Rook looked down at his feet and then at his surroundings. A city. Paris by the looks of it. He had been here recently, less than five years ago, on a mission for the Devil. He tore his gaze away from the elegant pale stone buildings with their lead grey roofs and fixed it back on Apollyon. "Open it."

"No."

He bared his fangs at the male. "Fine. I will open a portal then."

Although it required concentration, and he wasn't sure Apollyon would give him the time he needed to muster it even if he could get his mind off the fact he was in the mortal realm. Noises and scents swirled around him, and his thoughts dived down avenues that had him restless with the need to return to Hell before he surrendered to them.

Thoughts of Isadora.

Of finding her.

He needed to return to his own realm. Remaining here was dangerous. If he could feel his master's voice, the command to head back into Hell, he was sure he would be able to focus enough to cast his portal.

Why had his master stopped calling him?

Because the Devil wanted him to slay this angel for him?

He could do that. He would do it so he could go home and so his master would be pleased with him.

He readied his blade, gripping it before him with both hands.

"Just focus, Rook. Focus and see if you can find her." Apollyon's dark eyebrows furrowed. "She's in danger. A group of witches have her, one known to be stealing powers from other witches by killing them."

An inferno consumed him at the thought of the female in danger, more violent than the one that had gripped him the first time Apollyon had told him the witch was in trouble. He cursed himself, sure he had been feeding it by looking at her picture, by trying to see if he could remember her. He had given her power over him by thinking about her. She was a lie.

But what if she wasn't?

What if she was in grave danger and he was the only one who could save her?

Apollyon's blue eyes gained a glimmer he didn't like, one that said the angel thought he was reaching him at last.

"It has nothing to do with me," he bit out and swept his blade down at his side as he advanced on Apollyon. "I do not know the female."

"You do know her." The dark angel backed off a step. "You know her better than anyone."

He didn't believe that.

He charged at the angel on a roar.

Apollyon kicked off, launched backwards and spread his wings. He twisted and beat them, flew along the road low to the ground.

Rook gave chase, not because he was curious about the witch or because he believed a word Apollyon said, but because he was determined to take the male's head. The Devil would forgive him for leaving Hell unsanctioned if he brought back such a fine gift and Rook's life would be quieter for it too. He could forget about the female and focus on his mission to take command of the First Battalion.

He flew harder, gaining height to get a better view of the angel as he followed the road and could chart the male's potential course.

A cold feeling went through him when he noticed something.

The street was empty.

Cars lined it, but they were stationary and there were no humans to be seen.

He looked over his shoulder and frowned. The route back towards the point where he had exited the portal was the same.

He focused.

The entire area was empty of people.

His eyebrows knitted harder. No, that wasn't true.

There was one signature other than the angel's in the vicinity.

He looked ahead again, in the direction the angel was flying, and almost slowed as he sensed power.

Not angelic.

It stirred a strange feeling inside him, one he didn't understand because it had the backs of his eyes burning and a fire blazing inside him, a confusing mixture of agony and anger.

His eyes slowly widened.

It was magic.

He could feel magic.

His gaze darted over the buildings that lined the broad road, seeking the one who wielded it.

Ahead of him, beyond Apollyon, on the rooftop of the white townhouse at the end of the street, stood a petite female. Her blonde hair whipped around her shoulders, a long thick dark red coat hugging her slender figure, reaching her ankles.

It wasn't the witch from the picture.

An odd sense of disappointment flooded him.

Fury and desperation replaced it when he realised Apollyon was ascending, heading for the witch, and she was smiling at the angel.

There was something about that knowing smile that had Rook flying harder, desperate to reach Apollyon before he could make it to her.

She held her hands out to Apollyon.

Rook closed the distance down to inches and stretched for the male's boots.

Roared as the witch caught the angel's hands and they both disappeared.

His demonic form shifted over his skin as he turned in the air, snarling and growling through his fangs as he scanned the area for them. They were gone.

*Fuck.*

He couldn't return without the angel's head, not if he wanted to keep his own one.

Rook flew in expanding circles over the city, scouring it for the angel.

As he flew, a need blossomed and he struggled to deny it.

He did not want to find Isadora.

He didn't know the witch. Apollyon was wrong about that.

But what if he *could* find her?

What would that even mean? That he had once been her guardian angel? Apollyon seemed sure he had been, and that he knew her. Finding her was important to the angel.

She might be a key to something after all.

He slowly smiled.

She might be the key to capturing the angel.

If he could find her, he could use her as bait and could fool the angel into lowering his guard by gaining his trust.

It was worth a shot.

Rook focused as he flew, his mind on the witch. He built a picture of her in it, saw silver hair and eyes as blue as moonlight, a contrast to the way he had imagined her all the times he had studied the drawing of her. Her true appearance, or a new one his mind had constructed in an attempt to see if he really knew her?

As he reached the outskirts of the city, where it gave way to country roads and larger dwellings, something stirred inside him.

He followed the sensation that beat in his veins like a drum, changing course whenever it grew weaker, and flying harder whenever it gained strength. Was he closing in on her when that happened?

The day came and went, and his focus slipped at times, fatigue creeping up on him and forcing him to set down more than once in the countryside. It was impossible to rest though, even for five minutes. The sensation that he was getting closer to her and the drum that now pounded in his breast drove him to keep going, to continue searching and not stop for anything.

Not even if he fell from the sky.

Moonlight chased over the land below him as he flew, the air so cold it chilled his skin, and the scent of snow rose from the quiet white countryside. No sound other than that of his wings beating the night air reached his ears.

The entire world had fallen silent.

He blinked away sleep, ignoring the desire, and shut out the hunger gnawing at his stomach.

All that mattered was the beating drum, and that it was growing stronger, pulling him towards something now.

Lights in the distance caught his attention as he rubbed the exposed patch of stomach between his hip armour and breastplate, trying to silence his stomach. He could eat and rest soon enough.

He focused on the golden light, frowned when his eyes grew hazy and blinked to clear them. The cold wasn't doing him any favours. It sapped his strength, had his muscles sluggish and wings tiring faster than they should have been. He had flown plenty of times in the mortal world, knew his body's needs when he was in this realm. He should have been able to keep going a little longer.

He cursed the snow.

He couldn't remember the last time he had seen so much white. He wasn't sure he had ever seen it. He cursed the cold too, missed the heat of Hell as he swept lower, seeking warmer air.

Spires pierced the white glow of the mountains as he descended, almost silhouetted against them. As he approached the pale stone castle, the shadows shrouding it fell away to reveal conical and square towers.

He did a lap of the building, studying it as he flew over the snowy grounds, his stomach rumbling again. The chateau was occupied. He could probably get food inside, could slip in unnoticed to steal something to eat that would give him the strength to keep going.

He dropped lower.

Hit an invisible barrier that repelled him.

"What the fuck?" he muttered and beat his wings to hold his position in the frigid air as he stretched a hand out.

He slowly moved forwards until his palm met the invisible force. He pressed against it, his eyebrows pinching together as it resisted him, didn't even bow as he exerted all of his remaining strength on it.

Magic?

He scanned the dark brown tiled roof below him and what he could see of the inner courtyard of the stilted circle of the chateau.

Was she here?

He flapped his wings and flew higher, needing to get a better look at his surroundings. Mountains. A forest. A lake far up the valley to his right.

Not a single building other than this one for miles.

Whoever had cast the barrier liked their privacy.

Either that or they didn't want someone to know they were up to no good.

He wasn't one to judge those who were up to no good, because he had never been the hypocritical type, but it was hard not to when there was a chance these people had turned on their own kind.

As much as he wanted to climb the ranks, he had never actively taken down a fellow angel to achieve the upward motion he desired. He might have orchestrated a few of their deaths, but he had never done the deed. Plenty of angels in Hell were happy to do that for him. He just had to find whoever the angel he wanted eliminated had recently pissed off and point them in his direction.

Of course, some might view that as turning on his own kind.

Everyone had their own rules they lived by.

He flew around the perimeter of the barrier, studying that beat inside him, trying to discern whether it was growing stronger or weaker as he moved.

It grew stronger the closer he flew to the mountains.

Rook headed out over the forest and that unjustified sense of fury swept through him again as the beat grew weaker, confirming she was in the castle. He turned back towards it, glared at the towers and felt his eyes shift to crimson as black rippled over his skin.

New question.

Had the barrier been made by whoever had apparently taken her, or had she cast it to keep people out and protect herself?

He only had Apollyon's word to go on, and he didn't place much value in it. For all he knew, the angel could be luring him here so the witch could weaken herself by attempting to kill him and his own witch could steal her powers, making herself stronger.

Rook cautiously flew lower, touched down in the white garden and glared at his feet as they sank into the freezing snow. He shuddered and kicked his feet, trying to shake it off.

A golden light burst to life in the corner of his eye, near to the ground.

His eyes darted there.

A shadowy figure moved beyond the barred window.

Was it her?

Had he found her because he had been her guardian angel, or because this was all some elaborate trap devised by the angel and his witch?

He hadn't noticed the blonde witch casting a spell on him.

And the angel had seemed genuinely concerned about the safety of the one called Isadora.

He found himself wading through the snow towards that faint light, a need rising inside him, one so powerful he couldn't deny it, didn't feel the cold as the icy flakes washed over his knees and got into his boots. It consumed and controlled him, had him moving faster as it grew, driving him onwards. It beat inside him as fiercely as the feeling he was closing in on the witch in the picture.

Isadora.

He needed to see her in the flesh.

He needed to ask her a question, one that the answer to would either make him feel like a fool or turn his entire world on its head.

Did he know her?

# CHAPTER 5

Isadora focused her limited power on her right hand where she held it out in front of her, her palm facing upwards. Sweat broke out on her brow as she stared at it, her breaths shallowing and coming faster as she fought the spell that bound her magic. The incantation echoed in her mind, a low-level one she could normally cast without having to think about it. Now, it felt as if she was trying to cast something high-level, beyond her ability, and she feared her strength would give out before she could complete it.

Her limbs trembled, causing her hand to shake in the air before her, and her knees weakened beneath her, in danger of giving out as the minor spell drew on every drop of magic available to her, hungry for more.

She couldn't do this alone.

She closed her eyes, pulled down a breath to slow her racing heart, and shifted her focus to encompass a wider area.

She felt it the moment she connected with the ancient nature surrounding her. Power trickled into her. It would have been a torrent had it not been for her damned manacles.

But that trickle was enough.

Her eyes snapped open.

A tiny spark ignited above her palm as she channelled the magic into the spell she chanted quietly beneath her breath, afraid someone would hear her and stop her. Her heart hammered as that flicker of light became a small flame that weakly illuminated her hand.

Desperation drove her, had her pushing harder regardless of the potential dangers.

She could set herself on fire and she wouldn't care, not as long as she could cast the light far enough into the world outside her cell window to reveal whether she had been hearing things.

Or whether the sound of wings really had broken the eerie stillness of the wintry night.

The flame burned brighter, its light stretching to the walls now, and she nurtured it, ignoring the weakness building inside her to push it harder still.

A blazing golden orb burst into existence above her palm. It swirled and twisted furiously, the bands of bright yellow and deep orange twining together into a blur as it picked up speed.

She dialled back her magic, slowing everything down as she centred her mind so she could control the flames. The spinning orb decelerated, the bands reappearing again as they moved at a speed her eyes could track.

Isadora lifted her hands as she tiptoed, reaching up towards the window, careful to keep them level so she didn't drop the orb. Her right ankle wobbled beneath her and she swayed that way. Her eyes shot wide as her left hand jerked, the drop of her right one tugging on it, and she almost lost her grip on the spell. She stilled right down to her breathing, heart pounding as she stared at the fireball. The heat of it seared her, a reminder that if she dropped it, she was liable to injure herself.

"Stupid shackles." She glared at them.

The chain that linked them was short, making it difficult to use her hands. She could do this though. She grimaced as she eased up on her toes again, pressing her chest to the damp stone wall for support, and finally reached the window. She bit her lip and fumbled with the latch on the window with one hand as she struggled to keep hold of the fireball with the other.

The latch finally gave. She stretched higher, trying to push the pane up so she could hurl the flaming light into the garden, ready to utter the words that would cause it to flare up again and explode into a bright well of flames that would chase back the night.

Her tired muscles trembled beneath her skin as she struggled with the heavy window, aching as she tried to force the pane high enough. When her arm felt as if it would give out, she mustered all of her strength and grunted as she tossed the fireball as far as she could manage.

It made it barely eight inches before it landed in the snow with a sizzle.

"Dammit," she muttered under her breath and gripped the bars in both hands to hold herself up so she could see the orb.

She focused on it and it began to roll, hissing and throwing up steam as it carved a channel in the snow.

"Keep going," she murmured as she weakened again.

She willed the fiery ball to roll a little more. Just a few more inches. It was almost twenty feet from her now.

She readied the spell again, because she had to know if an angel had come for her. The hope the sound of wings had birthed in her was killing her. She wasn't sure she could take it if it had been her imagination.

The black-winged angel she had heard rumours about in Paris had to be Apollyon. It just had to be him. She swore she had felt his power too, familiar and comforting. His senses were sharper than hers. If she had felt him, he must have felt her. The reason the people holding her kept moving her had to be because Apollyon was looking for her.

She tried to suppress that hope as it ran out of control, afraid it really would destroy her if it was shattered. She couldn't tamp it down though. It seized her, gripped her so hard it was impossible to shake it and stop her mind from spinning with a thousand thoughts of seeing Apollyon again and the things he could tell her.

He would be able to tell her what had happened to Rook.

She stilled as the glow emanating from the orb cast light over a pair of armoured shins.

Not the gold-edged obsidian armour she knew Apollyon wore.

The edges were the colour of blood.

Armour belonging to the ranks of the Devil.

Her throat closed as memories surged to the surface of her mind to strip away all that was left of her strength. She clung to the bars with trembling fingers, stopping herself from collapsing, refusing to let this male see her weak and vulnerable.

Not a demonic angel.

They were betrayers. Devious and cruel. Vicious. They lusted after bloodshed and destruction, a gift from their master's poisonous temperament and his blackened soul.

They took pleasure from delivering pain.

Images of her own blood spilling on black flagstones stuttered across her eyes as his taunts rang in her ears, promises of relief if she gave him what he desired.

Her grip on reality began to slip.

Isadora forced herself to focus on the Hell's angel standing by her orb. She chanted the spell louder now, putting strength into each word, imbuing them with power.

This angel wouldn't take her.

She wouldn't go through that hell again.

She wasn't sure how the Devil had found her, but she would be more careful in the future. She would take this demon down so he couldn't report to his master and then she would reinforce her protective spells, the ones that had kept her concealed for centuries.

The orb blazed brighter, driving back the darkness, spewing streams of fire as it began to rotate, swiftly picking up speed as it grew in size.

The demon stepped back.

Isadora glanced at him, wanting to see his terror in the moment before she pushed the orb to overload and explode.

She froze.

Her legs gave out, swept from beneath her by the wave of disbelief that rocked her.

She hit the hard stone floor of the cell with jarring force and collapsed forwards, bracing herself on trembling arms.

No. She had to be mistaken. It wasn't possible.

She shook her head and wanted to laugh at herself for imagining such a ridiculous thing. Tears came instead, a flood of them that stole her breath, had her choking on sobs as her heart ached so fiercely she felt sure it would finally give out.

It wasn't possible.

"Mother Earth... please don't let it be possible," she whispered, her eyes and nose burning, throat tight as she fought the tide of her emotions, ones centred around the grief she had carried inside her for thousands of years.

Isadora mustered her strength, forced herself back onto her feet and clutched the rough stone wall, using it to haul herself back up. She needed to see if her mind had played a cruel trick on her.

Because it couldn't be him.

She leaned into the wall, reached up and gripped the bars of the window. The sound of her shackles clanking against them competed with the noise of her rapid breaths as she tried not to cry.

She lifted her head, daring a glance at the demonic angel.

He stood staring down at the orb that had shrunk in size and had almost fizzled out, his eyes a strange shade of gold with turquoise hints as the warm light emanating from it flickered across his face. His head canted left and his black hair fell forwards to brush his brow.

She charted the familiar sculpted planes of his face, from the strong line of his square jaw to his high cheekbones, and the straight blade of his nose. Jet eyebrows dipped, narrowing his eyes in that way she had always found sexy, and pain tore a sob from her.

Because her beautiful, noble angel had fallen.

And she was sure it had been her fault.

She shifted closer to the window, an apology balanced on her lips, one she knew would be inadequate. Nothing she said or did could make up for what had happened to him because of her. He loathed the demonic angels, despised Hell and everything it represented, had been fiercely loyal to Heaven and proud of his position there.

She ached at the thought of what he must have gone through, how it must have killed him to fall from grace and become something he had hated.

Isadora covered her mouth with her left hand, her eyebrows furrowing as she forced herself to look at him, to see it really was him.

It wasn't her imagination, a trick created by her fatigue and the hope she foolishly kept alive.

If he had been born of her imagination, he would have appeared as he had when she had known him. He would have been the angel she had fallen for all those centuries ago.

His hair would have been longer, his beautiful wings silver-blue instead of crimson, and his armour would have been cerulean edged with silver.

A need to touch him rushed through her, so she could be sure he really was there, was flesh and blood.

Alive.

She reached her right hand higher and tried to stretch it through the bars.

Her manacle clanked against the steel rod.

Turquoise eyes shifted to settle on her.

His black eyebrows pinched harder, putting a furrow between them above his straight nose.

He moved towards her, stepping over the orb, his eyes locked on hers. They were cold, flinty in a way she didn't like and couldn't understand. She stared up into them as he drew closer and she caught the flicker of anger that darkened them as he suddenly stopped.

He lifted his right hand and the skin of his palm paled as he pushed it forwards, as if it pressed against something.

A barrier.

The witches had cast a protective barrier over the castle.

Panic came rushing back, no longer born of fear a demonic angel had come for her. Now, it was born of the fact he couldn't reach her.

She squeezed her right arm through the bars and reached for him, desperate to make contact, to somehow shatter the barrier that separated them so he could get to her.

Those turquoise eyes dropped to her and grew colder, all emotion draining from them as he glared at her.

"Rook." She stretched for him, afraid he would leave now that he couldn't reach her.

His eyes widened and he shifted back a step.

Her reach for him had the opposite effect to what she wanted.

He was swift to turn on his heel, beat his wings and take flight, and she could only stare as he quickly disappeared into the night. Cold swept through her, not the frigid chill of the wintry weather but the bitter bite of despair and devastation. She sank to her knees, her hands falling into her lap, and stared at the stone floor as something hit her.

Rook didn't know her.

She shook her head at that. It wasn't possible. She was reading into things because she hated how cold he had looked when he had gazed upon her, such a stark contrast to the male who had always held heat in his eyes when looking at her before.

He knew her. He had to know her. He had been the one to tell her all those years ago about angels, about how he would lose his memories if he died and was reborn in Heaven. He had made it sound as if angels retained their memories if they fell.

"What do I know?" she muttered to her knees, then twisted and sank against the wall, sitting on her backside on the icy flagstones.

Was it possible angels also lost their memories when they fell?

She leaned forwards, buried her fingers in her fall of silver hair and clawed it back as she curled up into a ball.

It hurt.

It hurt to know Rook had been alive all this time.

Serving the very realm that had made her believe he was dead.

Fresh pain rolled through her, memories of that night bombarding her, a blur of rage and agony so deep it cut and lashed at her. Tears streaked down her cheeks as she held herself, desperately trying to keep herself together because she felt as if this was it.

She was finally going to fall apart.

She couldn't take any more.

Fear gripped her too, a poisoned whisper in her mind that grew louder as footsteps sounded in the corridor outside her cell.

She wasn't strong enough to withstand whatever they were going to do to her. She was too tired, too weak to endure it any longer. She would break.

Afraid that would happen, she did the only thing she could to protect the spell that bound her to Rook.

She muttered old words, ones that set her heart on fire and had her soul screaming in agony as she forced her magic to build inside her, fought the spell on the shackles and tapped back into the power of the nature surrounding her. Flames tore through her, shredding her strength, and she wavered, the world growing dark for a split-second before coming back. She gritted her teeth and pushed harder, desperate to muster the strength to cast the spell, a powerful one that was way beyond her ability while she was bound.

She had to do it though, even if it killed her.

She had to do it now.

If she didn't, she would give the witches everything they wanted.

The world darkened again, her head growing light as she fought to cast the spell. She shook off the dizziness and carried on, chanting the spell under her breath. Despair swept through her, stripping away all hope as she realised something.

She wasn't powerful enough to cast it, not even with a fragile connection to the natural magic in the forest and mountains.

She needed to be stronger. She needed a bigger boost.

Her eyes slowly widened as an idea formed, one that had her heart thundering against her ribs at a sickening pace.

Nature wasn't the only thing in the area she could connect with that had great power.

She closed her eyes and focused not on the world around her, but on herself, on her soul and the spell she was trying to protect.

A spell that linked her to Rook.

He couldn't have gone far, had to be close enough that she could make a connection with him.

The bond between them burst open and she gasped as power flooded her, what was probably only a fragment of what he had at his disposal but felt like a torrent in her weakened state. It lit her up, had every cell in her body buzzing as she struggled to get it under control.

"What are you doing in there?" London Town barked through the closed door.

She shut him out and focused as she chanted the spell again. She couldn't let him distract her. Distractions and potent magic didn't mix. The door rattled, the sound of metal scraping on metal making her pulse pound faster as she desperately tried to finish the incantation.

Pain lanced her mind as the spell took hold and she gritted her teeth as it burrowed into her, seeking the knowledge she wanted to forget.

The spell she had cast between her and Rook.

If she didn't know it, she would be safe. It would be safe.

And the world of immortals would be safe from a legion of witches who would try to use it against them in a power grab.

The door burst open.

Isadora jerked her head up.

Screamed and dug her fingers into her hair to clutch her skull as the spell went haywire, tearing through her mind, sending waves of white-hot fire shooting through her body.

Her heart thundered into overdrive.

Memories of researching the spell flashed into her mind and winked out of existence, but interlaced with them were memories of Rook. She tried to keep hold of them, scrambled and reached for them, but they slipped through her grasp, each one that disappeared leaving her colder and hollower inside.

"No." She shook her head and uttered the reversal spell, desperately trying to shut it down and stop it before it stripped all her memories of Rook from her.

The pain of seeing him again, of realising what had happened to him, coupled with the fact the binding spell involved him had left her memories of him open to the forgetting spell. A ripe curse peeled from her lips.

She should have realised it sooner, before she had recklessly cast it, so confident she could control it and keep her focus despite the draining effect of the shackles.

Now she feared it was too late to stop it.

More memories of him winked out of existence, ripping at her heart.

"Fucking hell." London Town sank to his knees beside her, gripped her wrists and chanted in time with her.

She twisted her hands and grasped his wrists, forming a stronger connection between them as she fought to stop the spell from taking everything from her.

She had been a fool.

All these years of wanting to forget Rook, of wanting her memories of him gone so she would be free of the pain of remembering what she had lost.

She had been wrong.

Her memories of Rook were precious, something she had always cherished despite the pain they had caused her.

She didn't want to forget him.

She gasped and jerked forwards as lightning struck her mind, a bolt so fierce it blinded her, turned everything white and made her ears ring.

When her vision came back, she was staring at London Town where he rested slumped against the dark stone wall opposite her, out cold.

Magic sparked around her fingertips like tiny bolts of electricity and she stared at them in a daze.

What had happened?

London Town groaned and rolled towards the floor, pressed his hands into it and pushed himself up as he shook his head. He clutched it, burying his fingers into his short mousy brown hair. "What the fuck did you do? You better not have forgotten that damned spell, you bitch."

He spat blood on the floor and lumbered onto his feet, swaying as he frowned down at the filthy wet marks on his black jeans and sweater.

Forgotten a spell?

Her eyebrows rose as she tried to remember what she had been doing. She recalled being pushed into the cell by Frenchie, vaguely remembered using magic, and then London Town had been with her.

Trying to stop her?

Perhaps she had forgotten a spell.

It must have been important to her.

She looked down and pressed her hands to her chest, surprised not to find a wet patch on the black t-shirt she wore.

Because she felt as if she had just carved out her heart.

# CHAPTER 6

Rook paced the small wooden chalet he had found deep in the woods near the lake, one that had seen better days. It stood at the foot of the mountains, shrouded by pines that must have closed in during the years it had been neglected. Snow rested heavily on the roof, causing the beams in the vaulted ceiling to groan at times in a way that had Rook tensing, sure it was about to collapse on his head.

He had spotted the rundown cabin when he had suddenly stopped flying and hadn't been able to convince himself to keep going.

That need to remain close to Isadora still lingered, tormenting him together with the questions that had been ricocheting around his tired mind all night.

Did he know her?

She had certainly known him.

Was it all a trick?

Maybe she was in on it. But if she had been pretending to know him, then she was a brilliant actress. He hadn't been able to stop himself from going to her when he had set eyes on her, when he had seen the tears that had streaked her cheeks glistening like rivers of diamonds in the moonlight.

When he had felt her pain.

Really *felt* it.

An invisible force had pulled him towards her.

Because he had wanted to take that pain away for her.

Even when part of him was sure he had caused it.

He wasn't familiar with witches, but every instinct he possessed said the golden orb she had created had been about to detonate until she had looked at him. The sight of him had truly shocked her, enough to send her dropping from view and to tear sobs from her. He had heard people cry before, but none of them had affected him like the sound of her choked sobbing.

She had sounded as if she had lost something precious to her, someone she had cared for so deeply that losing them had torn a part of her with it.

A piece of her soul.

No actress could manage such a feat.

No. Her pain had been real.

But that didn't mean she wasn't in on things.

Perhaps he had done something to the one she had loved, had been responsible for his death, and that was why she felt so familiar, and why the sight of him had hurt her so deeply.

He had killed many people in his years serving Hell, and a lot of angels too.

Was it possible she had loved an angel, as Apollyon's witch loved him, and Rook had taken that male from her?

Was this all an elaborate scheme to allow her to get revenge on him?

He growled and turned sharply when he reached the kitchen area of the small ski lodge, his boots loud on the wooden floor that creaked beneath his weight with each step. He paced back across the cramped room, passing between the stone fireplace that still stood to his right and what had probably been a couch or something similar before creatures and time had eaten it.

The air was musty, cold enough that his breath fogged as he unleashed another frustrated snarl.

He scrubbed his black hair and frowned, blinked hard to ward off sleep. He couldn't rest now. He wasn't safe here, not with the witches nearby.

He doubted he could sleep even if he risked it.

His mind churned with replays of Isadora, with visions of the beauty that had stolen his breath from his lungs. He had imagined so many things about her while he had stared at the drawing of her in his quarters, and half of them had been wrong.

The image of her that he had built in Paris when he had decided to search for her was correct though.

Her hair was silver like the moon.

Her irises were as bright as the light it spilled, a dazzling shade of pale blue.

He hadn't been able to get close enough to her to see her figure or her clothes, but he had noticed something else about her.

She wore shackles, and the dark score marks on her hands said she had worn them some time.

Because she was a prisoner as Apollyon had said?

She had appeared tired too, darkness circling her eyes and her skin sallow and thin.

Not an act.

He had sensed genuine fatigue in her, as if she hadn't eaten properly in weeks. Or was her weakness because the shackles she wore inhibited her magic? He had watched her struggling to push the orb towards him through the snow, had studied the toll it had taken on her and how close she had been to collapse at times. She had forced herself to continue though, revealing a strength that was alluring in a way.

The witch had fortitude, a resolve that many lacked.

He could admire that.

Rook paced around the dead couch and rolled his shoulders, trying to loosen up his tight muscles as a feeling pounded inside him, growing stronger with each beat and every thought that spun through his tired mind.

He couldn't leave her there.

Even if it was a trap, he couldn't ignore her plight. He couldn't just walk away and return to his life knowing she was the prisoner of someone, had been mistreated by them and might die because he hadn't saved her.

As heartless as his kind were meant to be, one still beat inside his chest from time to time.

An inconvenience, but one he endured.

So he would save her and then he would return to Hell, and he would forget about her.

He focused on himself, pushing through thoughts of her to fix his mind on ones of his realm and his master. He was sure the Devil would be calling him again, attempting to pull him back to Hell for punishment. He had disobeyed an order. That was grounds for execution. He had captured a few rogue Hell's angels in his time and had brought them before his master, had watched as the male utterly destroyed them, taking pleasure from exacting his punishment for their defiance.

He had thought it glorious at the time.

It didn't mean he wanted to be on the receiving end of it.

He pushed deeper, seeking the call he was certain would be there, subdued by how focused he was on the witch.

Only it wasn't there.

He felt no compulsion to return to Hell.

"The fuck?" he muttered and tried again but met with the same result.

The Devil wasn't calling him back.

His gut twisted at that, the bad feeling brewing in it again, the same way it had when his master had come to see what had been happening at the plateau. Back then, the feeling had driven him to conceal the picture of Isadora from the male. He still wasn't sure why. Something deep inside him, a feeling he couldn't quite make out, compelled him to keep her a secret.

Just as it compelled him to save her now.

Rook strode to the window, scrubbed the side of his fist across the dirty glass, and peered out at the thick forest and the sliver of sky he could see through the dark green canopy. That sky burned shades of copper and pink. The day was waning.

Night was coming.

He rolled his shoulders again, struggling to ease the tension building there as his body prepared itself for the coming fight. Not a fight. It would be a battle. It would take all of his strength to break through the barrier someone had placed over the chateau, leaving him weakened when he faced whoever was holding Isadora, vulnerable to their magic.

Victory would be his though. He wouldn't allow a few witches to stand between him and the female.

Whatever hits he took, he would keep pushing forwards, wouldn't stop until she was safe.

He wasn't sure he could stop even if he wanted to.

The need to save her was strong, controlling him as he opened the door of the chalet and stepped out into the evening. He strode forwards a few steps, into a clearing. Fire burned in his veins, rage that swiftly built from a spark to an inferno as he thought about Isadora in chains, enslaved by her own kind.

He growled and kicked off, shot into the air and spread his wings as he cleared the tops of the pines. He beat them to keep himself steady, twisted in the direction of the chateau and flew towards it.

Towards her.

The strange sensation she caused in him grew stronger as he closed the distance between them, creating an urge to fly faster, to reach her quicker. He pushed himself harder, ignoring the part of him that whispered to conserve his strength for the fight ahead. He couldn't. He needed to see the witch again.

He reached the chateau as the colours of evening drained from the sky, leaving the fingers of cloud cold against their darkening backdrop, as if someone had just sucked all the warmth from the world.

His gaze zipped to his left as movement there caught his eye.

A lone male.

A long black coat shrouded his slender frame and brushed through the snow as he walked the garden, smoke curling from his lips and the cigarette he held.

Rook halted in the air and narrowed his gaze as he assessed him. He had power. Rook could feel it as he focused, a low hum that matched the magic he could sense in the barrier. Had this witch created it?

Would such a barrier require more than one witch to cast it? If a group had been required to create it, would killing only one of them destroy it?

Hell, would killing this witch shatter the barrier if he had been the sole caster?

He wasn't sure of the answer to any of those questions.

He was sure of one thing though.

This witch was going to die.

Rook drew the crimson blade hanging at his waist and focused on it as he skimmed the flat of his right hand along it, transforming it into a broadsword.

He grinned and swept down towards the male, landed hard in the snow on the other side of the barrier, directly in front of the witch, and used his own type of magic to alter his appearance.

Normally, angels used a glamour to hide themselves entirely from mortal eyes or to conceal their wings and armour, replacing them with modern clothing so they could blend in with the humans.

Rook went one further.

It drained him, but it was necessary.

He needed to lure the male out from the protective sphere of the barrier.

The witch glanced his way when he moved along the edge of the barrier, pretending to be heading towards the woods that formed a boundary around the gardens of the elegant chateau.

"*Merde*," he muttered and started towards Rook, switching to English laced with a thick French accent as he hollered, "Stop there. How did you get out?"

Rook glanced across his shoulder at him, feigning shock and fear, manipulating the glamour with those emotions so the male would see it.

Or at least he would see Isadora looking at him with terror in her eyes.

Rook shuffled faster, clutching his hands to his chest, hoping the witch wouldn't feel the glamour as he neared him. He also hoped the bastard wouldn't see the sword he held point-down in front of him. Not until it was too late anyway.

He held back a grin as the witch crossed the barrier. He moved faster, limping towards the forest, luring the male there.

He glanced over his shoulder, checking the male was still following.

Ribbons of cerulean light twined around the witch's fingers as he closed in, and then stuttered as he suddenly halted just a few feet from him.

Damn it.

Rook lifted his gaze to the male's face and cursed again as surprise flickered in his blue eyes.

"Hang on a minute." The male frowned at him. "Where did you get those clothes?"

Rook didn't look down at the black dress he wore, one that hugged a figure he had imagined being sultry and sinful, curvy in all the best ways.

He pivoted on his heel to face the witch, lunged forwards and brought his blade up at the same time. His left shoulder slammed against the male's right one and he stared at the chateau beyond, at that tiny barred window in the basement where Isadora waited.

He was coming.

The male grunted, a rush of air leaving his lips in a cloud of white, and his eyes slowly widened.

Lowered.

Rook did grin now as he let the glamour fall away, allowing the male to see the crimson blade that pierced his chest as he took a step back and pulled it out of him.

Horror joined the shock in the witch's blue eyes as he watched the blade leaving him, all four feet of it.

When the tip left him, the male sagged to his knees in the snow and stared down at his knees and the pool of scarlet rapidly forming beneath him to soak into the white.

Rook swept his broadsword to his left, sending a spray of blood across the pristine snow there, and focused beyond the male to the chateau, and the barrier. It was weakening. The power that charged the air was fading as the witch's life bled from him.

He looked down at the male as he drew up beside him and then back at the castle. An image of Isadora in shackles, her delicate face gaunt and streaked with tears flashed across his mind. A low growl rumbled up his throat and his teeth sharpened in response, the rage in his blood rolling back to a boil as he shifted his gaze to the window where he had seen her last night.

He swung his blade and didn't look back as the witch's head thudded to the ground.

He strode forwards, flaring his crimson wings out and snarling as darkness chased over his skin, the urge to shift into his demonic form rushing through him as his mind leaped ahead to imagine killing the others who had harmed Isadora.

He didn't take his eyes off the window as he approached, couldn't drag them away as a need to see her pounded inside him.

The barrier was gone by the time he reached the point where he had stood last night and he grinned, flashing fangs, as he stormed right past it and closed in on the chateau. His senses stretched out, covering every square and conical tower on the ancient circular stone building. He counted five inside including Isadora.

Her signature was fainter now, weaker than it had been last night. Had they done something to her?

He moved to her window, needing to see.

She didn't appear in it as she had before. No light flickered to guide him to her or reveal her to him. He stopped when he reached the wall and hunkered down, not caring that his wings dragged through the snow. All that mattered was seeing Isadora again.

He set his sword down and angled his head so he could peer through the window.

It was dark in the small cell, but his heightened vision took care of that as he focused on the room.

Revealing Isadora.

She sat in the far corner to the right of the door, her eyes wide and glassy as she stared ahead of her.

What had they done to her?

"Isadora?" he murmured, wanting her to look at him but not wanting to draw attention to himself.

Not yet, anyway.

Part of him had been beginning to consider ripping a hole in the wall and just taking Isadora and running with her.

It wasn't an option now.

The hunger to spill blood, to kill every fucking bastard in the building blazed through him, gripped him and had him itching to fight as he looked at her.

As he saw the bruises that littered her face, neck and arms.

As she slowly lifted her head to look at him through hollow eyes.

They had tortured her.

He had seen it enough times to recognise it, but it had never made him burn like this, twisted tight inside with a need to avenge her.

"Isadora," he whispered and pressed his right hand to the glass that separated them. "It's me... Rook."

Her fine dark eyebrows twitched.

The recognition and relief he expected to fill her eyes didn't happen. They remained flat and cold.

"The fuck?" he growled to himself, and then softly said to her, "You know me."

Confusion put a furrow in her brow. "I know... no Rook."

# CHAPTER 7

The sound of Isadora's hoarse voice and the thought they had done something to her to make her forget him ignited a fury so deep inside Rook that he was flying over the chateau's roof before he had considered what he was doing.

He snarled and dived at the first person he saw.

The female crossing the courtyard didn't have a chance to react.

Her head toppled onto the snow-dusted cobbles before she could even gasp and he landed beyond her, furled his wings against his back and roared out his rage.

An older male burst out of the door ahead of him, took one look at the dead female, and fled, heading back into the building.

Rook grinned and beat his wings, shot towards the male and caught him before he made it more than two steps inside. He gripped the grey-haired portly witch by the nape of his neck, digging his claws in deep, twisted and slammed him face-first into the wall. The male choked out a grunt and Rook pressed him harder against the wall, until bone shattered beneath the pressure of his grip and he went limp in Rook's hand.

He cast the dead witch aside and focused on the building, seeking the others. The female and the older male had been dressed in the same style, crisp black trousers and a white shirt. Servants?

Were the two remaining witches in the chateau servants too?

He recalled what Apollyon had said to him. A group of witches had her. He doubted that the dark angel had meant one powerful witch and his servants. At least one of the remaining people would be as powerful as the one he had slain outside to make the barrier fall.

He mentally prepared himself for that as he stalked through the elegant sage-green kitchen and into a pale cream hallway. His heavy footfalls echoed along it as he tracked his next target, following a branch to his left. He reached a bright foyer and scanned the building again as he stilled and listened, seeking his prey.

A heartbeat, faint and distant, but closing in, sounded above him.

He looked up the dark oak staircase to the next floor. The lights were lower there, barely illuminating the wood-panelled walls. He canted his head to his left. The heartbeat was closer now.

Rook moved to the bottom of the staircase.

"I am telling you, I heard a noise." The female voice sounded harried.

"Now you're just making up excuses to get away from me." A male growled, his accent not matching hers.

He was British.

The dark-haired female appeared in view on the landing above Rook, her hands trembling as she wrestled with the buttons on her white shirt, hastily fastening them. "I will get into trouble if they know what we were doing."

Rook's nostrils flared.

She smelled of sex.

So did the mousy-haired male who was striding towards her, hunger still colouring his eyes as he kept them fixed on her.

The female stopped dead as her eyes landed on Rook.

The male grinned, swept up behind her and wrapped his arms around her. "I knew you'd change your mind."

His grin faded when she didn't respond.

"Ellie?" He leaned to his right, trying to see her face.

Rook waited.

Watched all the colour drain from her skin as she stared at him, her dark eyes gradually growing as round as the full moon outside.

The British male frowned and slowly shifted his gaze, tracking hers.

A slow grin curled Rook's lips as the male blanched.

"What the…" The male rallied, shoved the female aside and broke to his left, back the way he had come.

How noble of him to leave the female to fend for herself.

Rook casually ascended the stairs, his crimson wings brushing his ankles with each step, his eyes locked on the female as he tracked the male with his senses to make sure he didn't get away.

She sank to her knees, sobbing hysterically, the sound grating in Rook's ears.

He stooped, closed his hand around her throat, lifted her off the floor by it and held her before him. She flailed her legs and clawed at his arm, a weak attempt to break free of his grip. He tightened his hold on her and her fight left her. She stilled, tears streaming down her cheeks as she stared into his eyes, resignation filling hers, leaving them as hollow as Isadora's had been.

"Did you hurt Isadora?" he said and she tried to shake her head. "Do you have anything to do with what happened to her?"

Another attempted shake.

He sighed. "A nice angel would let you go and would only mete out justice to those who had hurt her, right?"

She nodded, a tiny seed of hope bringing life back into her eyes.

Rook set her down on her feet and released her neck to cup her cheek, his thumb brushing the other side of her jaw.

"Sucks for you that I'm not a nice angel." He shoved his hand up and forwards.

Bone crunched.

She dropped to the crimson carpet, landing on her back with her wide startled eyes locked on the ceiling, her mouth opened on the gasp that would never leave her lips.

No one in this chateau was innocent.

She worked for whoever had Isadora, which meant she had been involved, had known what sort of person her employer was and had done nothing about it. She had been fucking one of the males responsible for hurting Isadora. She was as much to blame as the rest of them.

He stepped over her body and stalked down the corridor, tracking the final witch.

The male's heartbeat hammered frantically, thundering in Rook's ears, driving him on. He grinned as he hunted him, following that rapid beat, and passed his hand over the length of his blade, shortening it this time, anticipating the coming fight. It would be close quarters, room to swing it limited despite the size of the apartments he could see on either side of the hallway.

While he preferred the length and power of his broadsword, he was just as comfortable fighting with a smaller blade.

The witch was going to find out just how comfortable he was with it.

His grin stretched wider as he closed in and detected someone in a room to his right, beyond a smaller dark wooden staircase that led both downwards and upwards.

Rook glanced down the steps as he passed it. Why hadn't the male escaped that way?

Perhaps in his blind rush to flee, he had missed the staircase in the low-lit hallway and had panicked, hiding in a room instead.

Perhaps he was lying in wait, ready to attack when Rook stepped into the room.

No matter.

He closed in on the door, the only one in the corridor that was shut. If the witch had wanted to hide from him, he should have left it open, making it appear like the others. This witch wanted to fight. He smirked at that. This witch was an idiot.

He was strong, but Rook was stronger. His build alone would have given him the advantage over the slighter male, but the powers he commanded combined with a thousand years of battle experience all but assured he would be the victor.

Rook lifted his right foot and slammed it into the door, sending it crashing into the wall. The sound of the collision echoed along the corridor as he peered into the darkness. Unusual darkness. He couldn't penetrate it, no matter how hard his eyes tried to pick out some details in the room.

Was the witch cloaking himself with the shadows?

The male's heartbeat still pounded in his ears. He had taken Rook's sight from him, but he should have doused all his senses. It was easy to pinpoint the male directly in front of him, at the far end of the room.

Rook prowled forwards, his fingers flexing around the black hilt of his sword.

Dazzling colourful light erupted around him and he flinched, reared back and snarled as he flashed fangs.

If the idiot meant to blind him…

Pain tore up his legs.

Rook roared as a thousand white-hot needles pierced his flesh in a rising wave.

He squinted against the bright light and looked down.

"Fuck!" He slashed at the thick thorny vines wrapping around his legs, hacking at their bases where they blended into the wooden floor before they could reach his thighs.

He growled as he reached down and ripped at them, tearing the long thorns from his flesh. Blood tracked down his legs from each puncture wound, leaking from him as he wrestled with the rest. They tangled around him, snagging him again whenever he managed to free himself.

Adrenaline surged in response, his heart racing as panic tried to grip him. It wasn't going to happen.

He roared and let the change come over him, watched as the skin on his legs turned black as his body began to grow, limbs thickening with muscle as the floor dropped away.

"Shit," the witch muttered and the colourful lights brightened, the vines growing faster in response.

Rook grunted as another thick onyx vine wrapped around his left leg, sinking thorns deep into his black skin. He glared at it and hacked at the root, managing to stop its growth. His crimson gaze scanned the vines that littered the floor around him, wilting now he had cut them. More sprouted from the wooden boards.

He frowned, his eyes snagging on something.

A pattern beneath the dead branches.

On a feral roar, he slashed his sword through the markings, carving a long groove in them.

The light stuttered.

"Oh, bollocks." The witch's pulse jacked up in his ears, the scent of his fear flooding the room.

Rook cut at the floor again, interrupting the spell that formed a circle beneath him. It began to fade, the vines that had been sprouting withering before his eyes. He staggered forwards, each step agony as the lacerations and punctures on his legs stretched and pulled, spilling crimson over his black skin.

The mousy-haired male appeared before him as the spell shattered.

He had his back pressed against the pale blue wall between a four-poster bed with rumpled navy covers and an antique wooden wardrobe.

"Wh-what do you want?" The attempt to sound confident and calm failed, and the male looked ready to soil himself as Rook closed in.

The witch clutched his hands together in front of his chest and swirls of purple and blue light streaked upwards from them. A sword formed in his grasp, silver and very elegant. Utterly impractical. It was whip-thin and had a fancy guard made of gold. Evidently, he had never fought with a weapon before.

"Is that meant to be a sword or a magic wand?" Rook jerked his chin towards it.

The male swallowed hard, his voice rising an octave as he bit out, "It's a fucking sword."

Rook smiled slowly. "This is a sword."

He swept his hand down his own weapon, took pleasure from the way the witch's skin paled and his eyes grew enormous as the blade transformed, growing to twice its original length and breadth.

Rook weighed it in his hands, still in love with the heaviness of it after all these centuries. It felt good in his grip. Always did. Always would.

He regarded it with a slight frown.

"You asked what I wanted." He lifted his crimson eyes to lock with the witch's. "I had wanted to ask you some questions. Like... why did you take Isadora?"

The male's expression shifted, the fear fading as he mistakenly saw an opportunity to bargain for his worthless life.

"You want her? Take her. It wasn't my idea. Who wants to be immortal, right?" His lips twitched in a smile that reeked of nerves. "Apart from you. Must be nice being immortal... but not my thing. I really don't want to be immortal."

Rook arched an eyebrow at that.

So Isadora was immortal.

"A spell did this to her?" He didn't wait for the witch to answer him, pieced together the answers in his head to build a picture of what had happened, one he didn't like. "You all wanted to know this immortality spell, so you captured her... and she didn't want to tell you... so you hurt her."

He advanced a step, a growl peeling from his lips as he imagined this male and the one he had beheaded outside laying hands on her, torturing her to make her surrender it.

But his brave witch had resisted them.

"Please, mate," the male drawled, looked at the sword in his hands and held it up at his side as he shrugged, both of his hands in the air. "It's all a big misunderstanding."

He couldn't see how that was possible.

"So, I did not just see Isadora with bruises all over her?" He advanced another step, relishing how the bastard squirmed as he tried to hold his smile and the acrid scent of fear grew stronger in the air.

"We didn't do that." The male eased back against the wall. "I swear. She was doing something when I went to feed her last night... a spell... she was making herself forget and I tried to stop her."

Forget?

Had she been so desperate to protect the spell these people wanted that she had used another on herself, one that would place it beyond her reach as well as theirs?

His eyes widened as he recalled the way she had looked at him and what she had said.

She didn't know a Rook.

She had made herself forget him.

That cut deep, cleaving open his heart for some reason.

"So you beat her?" he snarled and glared at the male, his anger at what she had done pouring out in his words as his emotions started to get the better of him, a thousand whispered taunts filling his mind to drive him into the darkness.

"No." The witch shook his head. "It backfired. The spell. It happens sometimes. Magical backdraught. It hurt her. I swear… it wasn't me."

Rook had heard enough.

"I said I *had* wanted to ask you some questions," he bit out and hefted his sword. "What I want now is your head."

He swung hard, burying the blade into the wall with the force of his strike. Blood spilled down the witch's black t-shirt in a waterfall, reaching his bare feet before Rook had even pulled his blade free and caused the male's head to fall. It rolled across the floor and under the bed.

Rook turned away, transformed his sword and wiped it on the bedclothes before sheathing it at his waist.

He closed his eyes and concentrated.

Only one heartbeat remained.

Isadora.

Had she really cast a spell to forget him?

His eyebrows dipped low as he thought about that, as a need flared inside him, a hope as foolish as those he had witnessed in the eyes of his enemies tonight.

He hoped that she hadn't.

He hoped the one he had just killed had been right and she had meant to forget the immortality spell and not him.

Rook laughed at himself, sure he was heading for pain far worse than what he had felt on realising she had forgotten him. His master's words rang in his head. He had heard the Devil say them centuries ago and they had stuck with him, echoed in his mind whenever he watched the souls in the prison begging for mercy, saw it ignite in their eyes a moment before the life in them died.

*Hope was for fools.*

If it was for fools, then he was the king of them.

Because Isadora had awoken a thousand hopes in him and all of them were pinned on her.

# CHAPTER 8

Rook's legs were killing him by the time he reached the door of Isadora's cell in the basement. He pressed his hand to the cold metal, sensing her on the other side. She was calm, still in a daze if he had to guess. Had the spell she had cast that had apparently backfired really caused her injuries?

Had that spell been to forget him or the immortality spell the witches had wanted to take from her?

He lingered, unsure of the answer, or how he felt about it if she had wanted to forget him. He thought back to last night, to how she had looked at him with bold warmth in her eyes that had bordered on affection and the way she had breathed his name with such need that it had shocked him and sent him reeling.

He had been king of the fools before this moment, because he had sought to convince himself that he was either a target of an act by her or her enemy, while a secret part of himself had dared to hope that the feelings that had shone in her eyes had been real.

And for him.

He blew out his breath. "Ah, hell."

He gripped the silver handle and pressed down, no relief filling him when it gave and the door opened a crack. All he felt were nerves that were foreign to him, a sense of unease that set him on edge as he gathered the courage to step into the room.

He drew down another deep breath and pushed the door open.

Isadora scurried away on her hands and knees, racing for the far corner, muttering to herself. Her manacles scraped over the stone, tearing at his black heart, and his eyes sought her. She twisted onto her backside and huddled up, forming a small ball, her silver hair like a waterfall in the moonlight, tangled and wild.

The connection he had felt with her burst back to life. The intensity of it damn near stole his breath as he stared at her and a deep ache formed inside him, a sense of longing that felt as if it had lasted centuries.

She was something to him. Something more than his ward?

He wanted to ask her that, but he held his tongue, because he wasn't sure he could take the thought of her saying again that she didn't know him.

He would get the answers he needed, but they wouldn't come from her. Apollyon would be the one he interrogated, because now he believed the angel had known him, and that he knew Isadora too.

Knew what Isadora had been to him.

"Isadora," he murmured softly, not wanting to frighten her. "It's time to leave."

She continued muttering to herself, strange words that held power. Was she trying to protect herself with a spell? From him?

He wouldn't hurt her. He wasn't sure he *could* hurt her. The thought of it turned his stomach, had him wanting to rage again, to unleash all the fury of Hell on this world, or maybe on himself if he dared to harm her.

He eased into the room and sank to his haunches in front of her, keeping his distance so he didn't scare her.

"Isadora?"

She stilled, her small body tensing, and then lifted her head slightly. He felt her gaze land on his boots and traverse his greaves. She stopped on his knees and he knew why. His skin was no longer black, his demonic appearance receded now, but blood from the puncture wounds covered him.

It didn't surprise him when she shrank away and muttered another spell.

"I won't hurt you." He carefully stretched a hand out towards her and she fell silent again. "I just want to take you away from here."

She shook her head. "The men…"

"Taken care of. The people who did this to you… they're gone, Isadora. I took care of them." Anger swelled once more to set his blood on fire, igniting a hunger to fight the males all over again, to draw out their deaths this time because it wasn't a spell that had reduced Isadora to a scared, timid little thing.

It was what they had done to her.

Things he didn't want to imagine because he was liable to go off the deep end again if he did.

"Let me free you." He reached closer to her. "I can remove those shackles."

She looked down at them. Shoved her hands towards him. His black heart ached all over again at the sight of her scarred wrists, at the dirt that covered them together with traces of blood, and all the bruises that littered her arms.

Rook shuffled closer.

He eased both hands towards hers, his focus locked on her, monitoring her for even the slightest sign that she was either afraid or about to attack him. She didn't know him and she had been through hell because of males. There was every chance she might panic and attack him as her instincts labelled him as a danger to her.

She tensed when he gently wrapped his hand around one of her cuffs.

"Not going to hurt you," he murmured, hoping to soothe her.

He wanted to chuckle at that. He had waged war for centuries, driven by the sole purpose of achieving power, uncaring of what he had to do to achieve it. How many lives had the hands he placed on her shackles taken? How many times had they been brutal and fierce, unyielding as they gripped his sword or the necks of his enemies? How many times had he used them to push unwilling mortals and demons into cells like this one?

He couldn't recall the last time he had touched something so gently, so carefully. Long ago enough that he was surprised he could remember how to be this tender.

His eyes settled on the cuffs.

A tender touch wasn't going to free Isadora from them though.

That required brute strength.

"I'm going to force them open." He hoped she understood what that meant, was lucid enough to comprehend that he wasn't going to hurt her, no matter how fierce he might appear.

She stared at him, dazed and not quite with him.

Was this really the result of a spell backfiring?

She looked as if she was no longer part of the world, was a bystander observing it all from a distance, removed from everything.

He wanted to lift his hand and brush her cheek to feel she was solid and real.

"Will it pass?" He focused back on her wrist and the first manacle.

It had no visible lock, but there was a hinge. Hinges were a weak point.

"Pass?" she murmured, slipping away from him again.

He could feel it as she retreated, floating further from his reach. Her eyes left him, drifting up to the window to his right.

"The moon is pretty tonight." A little sigh slipped from her lips.

Rook took her momentary distraction as a chance to break the first cuff.

He slipped his fingers beneath the band on either side of her wrist and bit back a growl as he pulled in opposite directions. The metal cut into his fingers but he ignored the sting as he gritted his teeth and poured every drop of his strength into breaking the shackle. His muscles bunched, straining and shaking, and he pushed harder, close to snarling as the cuff finally began to give.

It bent but didn't break.

The damned thing had to be magically reinforced.

"Fuck," he grumbled between hard breaths and looked at the oval of metal and then at her.

She stared at her arm.

"Can you squeeze your hand out?" Because he wasn't sure he could break it.

He didn't have the strength when it was bleeding out of him.

She nodded, her silver hair brushing the chest of her black t-shirt, and gripped the bent cuff with her left hand as she wriggled her other one, twisting it back and forth as she tried to slip it out.

A smile lit up her face when it popped free and her aqua eyes leaped up to meet his, sending a jolt through him that stole his breath and had him forgetting his pain.

Damn, she was beautiful.

Even with dirt streaking her face, dark circles around her eyes and bruises peppering her skin, she was breathtaking.

Stunning.

She flexed her fingers and turned her hand this way and that, her focus falling away from him to land on it.

He gripped her remaining shackle and gave it the same treatment, bending it enough that she had room to slip her hand out of it.

"Thank you," she whispered as he tossed the shackles aside, her gaze holding a hint of shyness as it met his and then flitted away.

"Let's get you out of here." He stood and held his hand out to her.

She eyed it, turned away and used the rough stones to pull herself onto her feet. He expected her to waver, to show a sign of the fatigue she had to be feeling, but she stood rod straight, resolve entering her eyes as she looked past him to the door.

She was heading towards it before he could even think about helping her, her steps steady but slow, cautious as she approached the hallway.

The spell wasn't the only thing that had drained her strength. He would need to get her something to eat.

He followed her, remaining close in case she needed him but not daring to butt in and help her without her asking or showing that she needed it. He was learning about her, and he was learning fast. She was liable to lash out at him if he took hold of her now, because she wanted to escape this place unaided, by her own volition.

Her own strength.

The very strength the witches had tried to strip from her with spells and starving her.

She had it in spades, every step she took stronger than the last. She gained confidence as she moved along the corridor, her heeled leather boots shuffling across the flagstones, enough that she released the wall and was walking without its support by the time she reached the staircase.

Her lean black-jeans-clad legs trembled at times as she slowly ascended them, clutching the railing for support.

She faltered near the top and he closed the distance between them, his gut clenching at the thought she might fall.

He stilled when she looked over her shoulder at him, her aqua eyes distant but holding a hint of warmth that rendered him immobile. She didn't know him. He reminded himself of that as he stared into those tropical eyes and that sense that he knew her returned full force to attempt to knock him on his ass.

She had known him once though, and maybe there was a chance she could know him again if he could find a way to break the spell she had cast on herself.

Could Apollyon's witch help with that?

Rook stuck close to Isadora as she mounted the final steps, there if she needed him, even if she didn't want him. She could be angry with him all she liked, all he cared about was keeping her safe.

Which was the most bizarre thing he had ever experienced.

He wasn't in the habit of caring for others.

He was second in command of the First Battalion, but he didn't give a damn about the angels under him. He didn't even give a damn about his commander. He only cared about himself, and most of the angels he had met in Hell were the same way.

But now he cared about someone else.

He hung back and watched Isadora as she crossed the foyer, heading in a direct line for the main door of the chateau, her pace quickening as she closed in on it and her freedom.

Her legs wobbled and he darted forwards a step, his heart in his mouth. She snapped them straight again, locking them and keeping her balance, and took another step forwards, this one more cautious.

He needed to help her get her strength back.

He glanced off to his right, towards the kitchen. She wasn't the only one who needed sustenance. His injuries were healing now, but they had drained him, and he needed his strength to return if he was going to cast a portal and get them to Paris.

He was sure Apollyon and his witch could help him with Isadora.

Rook looked back at Isadora, loath to leave her even when he knew they were alone. There wasn't a soul for miles in all directions. She would be safe. He tried to make that sink in. She *would* be safe and the quicker he made his way to the kitchen, the faster he could return to her, and hopefully he would be back before she ventured too far into the snowy grounds.

He strode towards the corridor on his right and a hot shiver raked down his spine as her eyes landed on him, dragging his focus back to her. He locked his senses on her as he rounded a corner, keeping track of her while he foraged for something they could eat.

The kitchen was further than he remembered, and he was glad that Isadora wasn't with him when he spared a glance at the dead male he had left near the courtyard exit. He had told her that he had taken care of those who had held her, but he wasn't sure she understood what that meant, and the thought she might react badly because he had killed someone sat like acid coated lead in his stomach.

Or maybe he was just hungry.

He snagged a bread roll from the box on the large wooden table in the centre of the kitchen and ate it as he found two bags, one of which had some apples in the bottom. He stuffed them with more bread, some meats and cheeses from a cold cupboard-like object that hummed and lit up when he opened it, and added some clear canisters of water.

Satisfied with his haul, he tied the handles of the bags together and hurried back towards the foyer.

Isadora was already out of the door when he reached it, and he stormed after her, tracking her with his senses. Relief washed through him to ease the turbulent churning of his stomach and the ache in his chest when he spotted her shuffling through the snow towards the trees to the left of the castle.

His pace slowed, steps arrested by the sight of her as the moonlight shone on her tangled silver hair and caressed her slender shoulders. With the mountains as her backdrop, and the stars shining in the inky sky above her, she looked ethereal, like something from another world.

An otherworldly creature who was rapidly closing in on the forest while he was struck dumb and staring at her.

"Isadora," he hollered.

She whipped to face him.

Fell right on her backside in the snow, sending a wave of it outwards from her as she sank into it.

"Damn. Sorry." He jogged over to her, caught her wrist before she could protest and pulled her back onto her feet.

She stumbled towards him, planted her hands against his crimson-edged black chest piece and stared up at him, the moonlight playing across her face in an entrancing way now, stealing the colour from her eyes.

Her breath fogged in the freezing air as she gazed up at him. Her pupils slowly dilated to devour the blue of her irises.

"I… ah…" He fought to keep his eyes on hers, battled the urge to look at her mouth as the feel of her slender body against his, her breasts and belly pressing into his exposed stomach, roused a fierce desire to kiss her. He awkwardly lifted the two bags he held. "I found food."

Cold washed over him as she tore her eyes from his to settle them on the bags, stealing the heat of her gaze from him.

"We should keep moving." He looked down at her clothes and the snow that covered them, already melting into the black material.

She would get sick if they lingered in the freezing night.

The thought of her falling ill sent a shockwave of emotion rolling through him, a potent mixture of concern, determination and resolve.

He mentally braced himself for her outrage, bent at the knee and scooped her up into his arms.

# CHAPTER 9

Isadora felt fragile in Rook's arms, terrifyingly breakable as he gripped her ribs and knees. A deep need to wrap her in his wings and shield her from the world ran in his veins, commanded him to keep her safe and do whatever it took to protect her.

She wasn't weak though.

He could feel the power in her, stronger than before now she was free of her shackles. It hummed inside her and into him through where they touched, a buzzing that felt like a warning to him.

One that was rapidly building.

"Put me down." She stared at his hand where he gripped her knee.

"Not going to happen." He took three strides through the deep snow and kicked off as he spread his scarlet wings and beat them, lifting into the air.

"Where are you taking me?" she snapped as her arms looped around his neck and she curled up against him.

Fuck, that felt too good.

He held her closer, calling himself a bastard for taking advantage of her like this, when she was afraid and in need of comfort.

"I found a place to stay, out of the way. We can rest there and then we'll head to Paris." He scouted the route ahead of them, charting the mountains and the trees, making sure they didn't have any company.

He wasn't sure the Devil would send men to retrieve him, or whether other witches might be in the area and see him taking Isadora, but he wasn't going to risk it.

He wasn't going to risk her.

If he spotted anyone en route to the cabin, he was taking them down.

"Paris," she breathed, her voice distant again, losing the strength that had been in it just moments ago.

Was she slipping back into her daze again, or just thoughtful? He wanted to glance at her, but he had always found it hard to fly and focus elsewhere. He tended to go in the direction of his gaze when that was happening and he was sure she wouldn't appreciate it if they suddenly dropped a few feet because he had been looking down at her.

"You don't remember me... but do you know an angel called Apollyon?" He couldn't stop his gaze from flitting to her as he asked that, unable to deny the need to see her reaction to that name.

She perked up again and pulled a thoughtful face, was silent for a full minute before she uttered, "Apollyon. I know that name. I know him."

For some reason that really pissed Rook off.

She had forgotten him, but she could remember the other angel. He silenced the voice at the back of his mind that hissed this was all a trick, an act to lure him into a trap, because he honestly didn't believe that anymore. If they had wanted to kill him, he had given them ample opportunities to take him down.

"You don't remember me though?" He couldn't stop himself from asking that, from wanting her to remember him and not because he wanted to ask her questions about himself.

Hell, maybe in part it was because he wanted her eyes on him again too.

It worked, because she gazed up at him, reigniting that warmth that had flared to life inside him when she had been pressed against him in the snow.

He banked right, spreading his wings to carry them effortlessly across the lake, towards the far side of it.

Her gaze lingered on him so long that he wanted to look down at her, felt a soul-deep need to stare into her eyes again and get lost in them. Maybe she was casting spells on him, making him want her.

Impossible, since she didn't need a spell to make that happen. He had yearned for her from the moment Apollyon had given him the drawing of her.

Not impossible. She could have cast a spell on him centuries ago, when she had apparently known him. There was a chance it would still be in effect.

Maybe she was the reason he couldn't recall things about his past, about the early years of his life in Hell and what had come before. Forgetting spells were in her repertoire after all.

"I'm sorry," she murmured quietly. "I don't remember you."

"That's alright." It wasn't, not by a long shot, but he didn't want her feeling bad about it.

He shook his head at that. What was she doing to him? He was a battle-hardened warrior, a black-hearted and vicious demonic angel who only cared about climbing the ladder in the Devil's ranks.

He risked a glance at her, unable to stop himself.

Maybe climbing that ladder wasn't the only thing he cared about anymore.

He was beginning to feel he cared about her.

Her eyes widened and she gripped his breastplate. "Pull up."

He growled and dropped his feet, beat his wings as trees came at them fast and cursed himself for getting distracted by her. His boots collided with the top of one of the pines and he struggled to avoid hitting it with his wings, twisted away from it as best he could and flew harder. The trees dropped away again.

"Mother Earth! Is this your first time flying?" she bit out, a hefty dose of sarcasm and bite in her voice that he found he liked.

He scowled at her. "No. I just didn't see them."

Because he had been too busy staring at her.

Was still too busy staring at her as they collided with another tree.

Rook pulled her against him and grimaced as they crashed through branches that restrained his wings, making it impossible for him to use them. He fumbled with one hand, trying to grab hold of something other than Isadora, and cursed as the branch he managed to snag slipped through his grip and they dropped together. His back struck a thick branch, knocking the wind from him, and he grunted as they rolled, falling towards the next one.

This wasn't going to go well.

He growled as he wrapped both arms and his wings around Isadora to protect her. She squeaked, her heart thundering in his ears as her fear flooded him.

He swore to the Devil they hit every damned branch on the way down, and every jagged broken one stuck him in his legs, his back or his wings, sending fresh fiery pain rolling through him. He twisted beneath her as they cleared the branches and spread his wings, trying to slow their ascent.

His breath left him in a rush as his back slammed into the earth and Isadora ploughed into his stomach, landing on top of him.

He closed his eyes, his wings stretched out at his sides, his right one bent at an awkward angle against the trunk of the pine that had just massacred him, and just lay there. He would move in a minute, when he could breathe again and the pain ricocheting through him faded.

Isadora wriggled in his arms, rubbing against him in a way that fired him up and flooded his mind with thoughts he really shouldn't be having given the situation.

"Are you alright?" Her cold palms framed his face as she moved so her body was flush against his, pressing down on it in a damned delicious way.

He nodded but kept his eyes closed.

She huffed, shoved up and sat astride him, and he had to bite back the groan that rumbled up his throat and wanted out. She had to know what she was doing to him sitting like that, her hands pressing against his bare stomach, scalding him despite their coldness.

"You need to learn how to fly," she snapped.

His eyes shot open and he fixed them on her as his eyebrows dipped low, the corners of his mouth turning downwards. "I can fly. I was just distracted."

"Distracted?" She tilted her head, causing her silver hair to shift across her breasts, and he squeezed his eyes shut before she distracted him all over again.

He wasn't going to answer her question. Evasion was the best recourse. The last thing he needed was her being aware of what a serious distraction she was and how he couldn't concentrate for shit around her.

"Are you hurt?" He mentally checked himself over, charting all the new puncture wounds on his legs, the shattered bone in his right wing, and the hole in his side that was leaking blood.

"No." Her gaze raked over him. "Are you?"

He chuckled at that. "I just hit every fucking branch in that tree and you need to ask me if I'm hurt?"

She scooted off him and he opened his eyes, pressed his elbows into the dirt and pushed himself up on them so he could see her. Her blue eyes skimmed over him, growing wider as they reached his legs.

"You're bleeding." She was definitely growing more lucid, and he liked it, not because he had been worried about her when she had been lost in a daze but because he liked the sound of her voice.

It was smooth like honey, took the edge off his mood whenever it caressed his ears, and quietened that niggling inner voice that kept telling him he was going to get into serious trouble for helping her.

"No shit." He sat up, not sure whether he was talking to her or that inner voice. He focused and waited for his wings to shrink into his back. They were reluctant to go, but he needed them away so they would heal and not cause him pain. He had enough of that to deal with. When they were gone, he clutched his right side, stemming the flow of blood, pressed his free hand into the earth and pushed himself onto his feet. "I was bleeding before I took a tumble through a tree."

She averted her gaze. Ashamed? Because he had been hurt rescuing her? It hit him that she was like him. She didn't like not being able to take care of herself. She didn't like being weak and having to rely on others.

"It's nothing I won't heal." His mouth twisted in a grimace as he moved and every muscle ached in protest, the wounds stinging as they pulled.

She moved towards him anyway, closing the gap down to only a few inches, and lifted her hands. She hesitated, drew down a swift breath and placed her palms against his stomach.

He tensed. "What are you—"

"Shh," she murmured, her brow furrowing as her eyes closed, and heat flowed into him, pleasant at first.

Until it reached the wound in his right side.

It gathered into a white-hot pool and he growled through his gritted teeth as pain arced through him, bolts of it shooting outwards from the wound. He loosed a string of obscenities, unable to clamp his jaw tightly enough to contain them as the fire built and spread, attacking other wounds on his body. He was glad he had sent his wings away, because he could well imagine how painful it would be to have her spell fixing them. It felt as if it was ripping him apart to put him back together again.

Isadora swayed towards him, her silvery eyebrows pinching, and her hands shook against him.

"Enough," he barked and stepped back to break contact when she didn't move.

He caught her arms when she fell forwards, stopping her from hitting the dirt, and held her upright. Her rapid breaths fogged in the icy air, her skin paler than before, and he wanted to rail at her, to curse and shout and demand to know why she had hurt herself in order to heal him.

But he couldn't, because he already knew the answer.

She felt responsible for what had happened to him.

So rather than barking and snapping at her, he settled for murmuring, "Thanks."

"I can do more," she whispered, breathless, her voice barely there.

He shook his head. She had exhausted herself by healing the worst of his wounds. He didn't want her to attempt to heal the others, not when he felt sure she would collapse if she tried. It would only flip their roles, making him feel responsible for what had happened to her. He felt responsible for her enough as it was.

"Can you stand unaided?" He kept his voice low, hoping it would sway her into forgetting about healing him.

She snatched her arms back, horror flashing across her pretty face as she stared at his outstretched hands. Had she only just noticed he had been holding her? An equally as pretty blush followed, staining her cheeks and bringing some colour back into her complexion.

He was right about her. She didn't like being coddled. She didn't like relying on another's strength.

Tough shit for her, since she was going to have to get used to relying on him for a while.

Starting with him providing for her.

He scanned the forest floor for the bags he had lost during the fall and huffed as he found one had ended up torn open, some of its contents scattered across the dirt, useless to them now. The other was dangling from a branch several metres up, a bread roll poking out of a tear in its side. He couldn't let his wings out again, not without damaging them further, so he leaped up, gripped a low branch and hauled himself into the tree.

Isadora's gaze followed him as he moved from branch to branch, stealing the pain from his body as it heated him. Or maybe it was the lingering effect of the spell she had funnelled into him.

He grabbed the bag, gripped the thick branch it had been hanging from and dropped. He swung and let go, falling to land in a crouch on the leaf litter beside Isadora.

She tensed when he rose to his full height before her, her blue eyes widening slightly as they locked with his.

He stared into them, mesmerised by how the moonlight changed their colour, making them colder despite the banked heat that flickered in them.

When she began idly rubbing at her bare arms, he shook himself free of the spell she had placed on him and jerked his chin towards the woods beyond her. "It's not far to a place we can rest." His gaze fell to her again as she looked over her shoulder in the direction of the chalet. "We need to get you warmed up."

Because as far as he knew, witches could get sick, and she was wet from her tumble in the snow. Coupled with the fact she needed nourishment, there was a high chance she would get ill if he kept her lingering in the cold much longer.

When her eyes finally roamed back to him, they were duller than before, and he could almost see her slipping away from him again.

He didn't want that to happen. "Isadora?"

She blinked at him but didn't respond. Her eyes fell to her wrist and she grazed her fingers over them, a distant edge to her gaze. What was she thinking in there? He wanted to ask her but he wouldn't get an answer.

Her pale fingers pressed against each bruise on her arms, and the thin lacerations that streaked up them from her wrists.

"You did a spell," he murmured, not sure if she knew what had happened to her.

Her eyes leaped to his and then dropped back to her arms. "Spell."

A crinkle formed between her eyebrows.

"I think it made you forget me." He pushed those words out, ignored the pain they caused as they fell from his lips, hung in the silent night and lingered, awaiting her response.

She looked at her arms, holding them out in front of her, and then tilted her head back and sighed. "I can't see the moon."

He shoved the disappointment down before it could surface and took hold of her left arm, carefully cradling it in his hand. She was cold, chilled to the bone, trembling beneath his touch.

"Let's get you warmed up." Because maybe it would make her more lucid again.

He wanted her back with him.

He started walking but she didn't move. He looked over his shoulder at her and tugged on her arm. She glanced at him and her eyes lingered on his, and fuck, he hated how far she was from him, shut away in a place he couldn't reach.

It had an ache forming in his breast, one he didn't want to understand, or acknowledge. She couldn't mean something to him. She just couldn't. He would take her to Paris, and then he needed to return to Hell, and face whatever punishment his master had in store for him.

He couldn't fall under her spell.

"You can see the moon better from the cabin." That seemed to break through the fog that surrounded her mind and she started walking.

He led her through the woods to the chalet, opened the door for her and guided her inside before she could even think about lingering outside to look at the moon. He would let her see it once she was warmed up.

He settled her on the floor by the fireplace and set the bag of food down next to her. Her eyes tracked him as he moved around the cabin, as he broke apart some of the wooden furniture to form kindling and gathered some logs that had been left beside the hearth.

It had been decades since he'd had to make a fire, but he could remember the basics enough that he had a blaze going before long. He stoked it with the rusted tools, trying to ignore the way Isadora's gaze burned into him, had him hotter than the flames that flickered and danced on the grate before him.

She shuffled closer and held her hands out to the flames. A little too close.

Rook grabbed her wrists to ease them back.

"Get off me. Don't touch them!" she barked as she twisted her arms free of his loose grip.

She shoved at him, knocking him on his backside, and scrambled away, breathing hard, a wild look in her eyes as they darted around the room.

She was looking for an escape route.

His heart lurched at that.

"Isadora," he murmured softly and held his hands up at his sides, hoping to calm her. "I wasn't going to hurt you. I just… you were too close to the flames."

Her chest heaved beneath her black t-shirt as she breathed faster, panic flaring in her blue eyes.

"Cannot let you see," she muttered under her breath and began rubbing at her forearms. "Cannot let anyone see. They'll come for me again."

He frowned. "Who will come? The witches?"

She rapidly shook her head, her eyebrows knitting hard. "Demons on dragons wings."

Cold swept through his veins, numbing every inch of him.

Hell's angels.

He sank back on his ass. His kind had targeted her before? Why?

He needed to know, but he wasn't going to get answers from her. She wrapped her arms around her knees and began rocking, shaking her head, her eyes on the fire. Foreign words left her lips, whispered quietly, so low he couldn't make them out, but he could feel the power in them as it flowed around him.

It was familiar.

She was so afraid that she was trying to shield herself, to form a protective bubble similar to the one the other witch had cast.

She was terrified of his kind, more than she was of witches, and damn, he wasn't sure how to process that.

It certainly screwed up his plans. He had intended to cast a portal to take them to Paris but he couldn't now. He wasn't sure whether she knew what powers a demonic angel possessed, but he wasn't willing to risk her freaking out on him and painting him in the same light as the ones who had evidently traumatised her.

Angels who had been after the same secret as the witches?

He focused and produced a blanket, a soft fluffy beige one that would be enough to warm her as she sat by the fire. She didn't acknowledge him as he carefully placed it around her shoulders. She kept chanting and staring at the flames.

He fixed food for her, turning the bag inside out and setting what he hoped was a suitable meal for her out on it.

"You need to eat." He unscrewed the cap of the water bottle, placed it beside her food, and picked up the sandwich.

She took it from him, her gaze following his hand, tracking it when he moved to sit beside her and grabbed his own sandwich.

He kept his eyes away from her, unsure whether she would react badly if he stared at her. Was it better to let her look at him, to pretend he didn't notice the way her eyes lingered on the cuts on his thighs and the remaining ones on his stomach? He wished he could pretend he didn't notice the way he burned wherever her gaze touched, his skin heating and a hunger rising within him, a need to have her hands on him again.

Her eyes reached his shoulders. "You're an angel."

His gaze leaped to meet hers and he lowered his sandwich from his lips without taking a bite, an unsettling feeling running through him as he waited for her to say something else, something he feared.

Did she know Hell's angels flew on crimson wings when they weren't in their demonic forms?

"You have wings." She took a small bite of her food, chewed and swallowed it. "What colour are they?"

He didn't want to answer that, so he bit into his own sandwich. It tasted good, the combination of meat and cheese quite pleasing, and his stomach growled for more.

Isadora's soft voice filled the silence.

"Silver-blue."

Rook stilled.

He hadn't had wings that colour in a long time, if Apollyon was to be believed and he had been a guardian angel in his former life.

His gaze drifted to her, and that feeling hit him again, that sense she was the key to unlocking his past and that Apollyon was right about them.

He had known her, had been something to her.

Something that left him shaken to his soul and conflicted, confused and unsure of himself as he stared at her, because whoever he had been, he wasn't that male now. He was something else, something she would despise if she knew.

He wasn't her guardian angel anymore.

He was her Hell's angel.

Would she still look at him with heat in her eyes if she knew that?

Or would she run from him?

# CHAPTER 10

It was freezing.

Isadora huddled deeper into the blanket wrapped around her, savouring the warmth as she tucked her legs up to get her icy feet under it. Her knees knocked against something solid. Was she facing a wall?

She pulled a face and rolled over, because she had stared at walls enough to last a lifetime since the witches had taken her captive.

A hazy memory formed, a notion that she was no longer held in a cell, was no longer a prisoner.

A heavy arm draped over her waist.

Her eyes widened as she looked down at the large hand that pressed against her stomach and pulled her back, drawing her against the solid form she had mistaken for a wall.

They widened even further when she realised that the soft blanket that warmed her wasn't a blanket at all.

It was a wing.

An image of the black-haired warrior popped into her head, together with a disjointed replay of what had happened

He had rescued her.

He murmured something in his sleep, sighed and dragged her closer still, so the hard planes of his body pressed into her back.

Heat flashed through her.

Panic followed it.

Isadora burst from his embrace, shooting to her feet to stand on the other side of the room to him where he remained on the dirty wooden floorboards.

Mother Earth, he was handsome.

Even more so than she recalled.

He smacked his firm lips together, a furrow forming above the straight line of his nose as his eyebrows knitted. That frown deepened as he moaned and fumbled, hand searching the dusty floorboards beside him.

For her?

She swallowed hard and fought to contain the heat that wanted to burn her cheeks over the fact she had been sleeping tucked against him, held close in his strong arms, shielded by his crimson wings.

It had been for the shared body heat.

That was the only reason she had been snuggled up against a male who was practically a stranger to her.

His searching hand reached the point where her head had been and roamed away from him. When he didn't find her, his eyes popped open, sharp and focused as they fixed on his hand and then scoured the room.

They stopped on her boots and skimmed up her legs.

She told herself to move, to do something to evade his gaze that was bringing fire up from her toes, flames that would scald her cheeks and reveal the fact he affected her.

It wasn't right to let him fluster her, to enjoy the feel of his eyes on her, and the hungry way they darkened, their tranquil turquoise depths turning stormy as they lingered on her body.

No. It *was* right.

She just wasn't sure why.

More than once, he had said that she knew him. She didn't remember him though, and she was sure she would recall such a noble, handsome male if she had met him before.

His deep voice rang in her mind.

She had done a spell to forget him.

Why would she want to do that?

Why had he seemed pained by the fact she couldn't remember him?

"You know me?" she whispered, cleared her throat and found her voice, because she was damned if she was going to break. She had to stay strong. She just couldn't remember why. "You said I knew you… so you know me."

He pushed up into a sitting position, his handsome face shifting in a grimace as he tilted his head one way and then the other, and stretched his wings. His right one, the one that had been draped over her, only extended a short way before he stopped, a twist to his lips that spoke of pain.

A mirthless chuckle left those lips. "I think we both forgot some things."

"I don't understand." She cautiously inched a step closer to him when he moved onto his knees and piled tinder and logs onto the grate in the fireplace.

He shrugged his broad shoulders, shifting his wings with them, but their bright crimson feathers didn't hold her attention this time. It was arrested by something she had failed to notice before, but couldn't miss now as she stared at him.

His breastplate was missing, revealing the chiseled perfection of his torso, from the wide flat slabs of his pectorals to the delicious ropes of his abdomen.

He glanced at her out of the corner of his eye.

Isadora averted her gaze, studying the fireplace. It had seen better days, looked as if it might crumble at any moment, much like the rest of the cabin.

"I don't understand either." He picked up a piece of wood and a stick, drawing her focus back to him.

Was he going to do what she thought he was going to do?

Her eyebrows lifted as he set the wood down and positioned some dried material in a hollow in it.

"Here, let me." She moved and was beside him, close to him, before she realised what she was doing.

Her arm brushed his. Lightning arced along her bones, a hot shiver chasing in its wake.

His dark turquoise eyes burned into her profile and she kept her gaze on her work, forced it to stay away from him and her focus to remain on the logs on the grate. She whispered the words, a basic spell that all witches learned at a young age.

The angel's gaze zipped to the logs as they caught ablaze.

He stared at them and she couldn't stop herself from looking at him, from tracing the noble lines of his profile and absorbing the way the flames danced in his eyes like the fires of Hell.

A chill skated down her spine and ice crawled over her skin, sending a shiver through her and igniting an urge to run. Why?

What was it about this angel that had her wanting to run away at the same time as she wanted to run to him?

"I'll make more food." He stood and she tracked him as he moved around the dilapidated cabin.

He looked troubled as he stopped near the dirty window and gazed out at the woods. They were thick, ancient. She could feel the power in them as it flowed around her and into her, restoring her strength.

She dropped her gaze to her wrists.

Strength that had been stripped from her by shackles this warrior had removed for her, granting her freedom she had been sure she would never taste again. He had saved her, had carried her to this secluded place and fed her, and had warmed her when the fire had gone out.

He had taken care of her.

"Why?" She locked gazes with him when he turned to look at her, a puzzled edge to his expression. "Why save me?"

He frowned down at his boots.

"Because I was asked to… because you knew me and I thought you could answer some questions…" He lifted his gaze to meet hers again. "Because I wanted to."

"Who asked you?" It seemed the safest one to start with.

"Apollyon." He shook his head, causing rogue strands of his black hair to fall down and caress his brow. He swept the tousled lengths back and loosed a sigh. "He tricked me into leaving… ah… chasing him and I ended up seeing if I could find you."

"Because you don't know me." She was sure he had wanted to say something else, something other than 'chasing him', but he had stopped himself.

Another why popped into her head.

"I don't know… maybe I do and I forgot." He cast his gaze towards the window again, blatantly avoiding her as he muttered, "At least I didn't choose to forget."

Had she?

The bite in his tone made it clear he believed she had chosen to forget him, had cast a spell on herself to erase him from her memories. Why would she want to do such a thing?

She looked at the healing marks on her arms, bruises that told her she had used a powerful spell and it had backfired. "It's possible I wasn't trying to forget you."

He turned fully to face her and planted his backside against the decaying cupboards of the kitchen area, a formidable sight with his crimson wings framing him and the scarlet-edged black armour that protected his hips, shins and forearms. The honed muscles of his chest only made him look more like a dangerous warrior, a deadly male who could handle whatever life threw at him.

Anything except her apparently choosing to forget him.

His eyes remained cold, constructing a wall between them that she had a strange urge to breach, one that left her feeling shut out when she had been welcome before. She wanted to be welcome again.

Not because he was the only one with her and she didn't want to be alone.

The reason eluded her, slipped through her fingers whenever she thought she had it, leaving her muddled again. Was it the spell that stole it from her? If she could figure out what spell she had cast, there was a chance she could reverse it.

"What do you remember about me... about the spell?" She rose onto her feet and crossed the room to him, aching to breach that barrier he had constructed and unable to deny the need to be close to him again.

She had seen witches who had forgotten things in the past, had witnessed how confused it had made them, especially when their instincts drew them to something and it went against everything their altered mind felt was right.

She had known this male.

Rook.

Isadora focused on his name, chanted it in her head as she gazed at him, as she stared so deep into his eyes that she was lost, unaware of the world as she drifted towards him. Her hands moved of their own volition, rising to frame his face in her palms, and it felt right.

Had she wanted to do this to him before?

Had the unfulfilled need lingered and now it was coming to the surface, her soul recalling her desire and acting on it?

He gazed down at her, tilting his head towards her as she held his cheeks.

"Do I know you?" she whispered, desperate to know the answer, to have her soul scream it at her and awaken from whatever terrible curse she had placed on it.

"Do I know you?" he murmured, echoing her, and darkness rose in his eyes.

A terrible grief rolled through her, tearing at her soul and closing her throat, causing the backs of her eyes and her nose to burn.

She couldn't breathe.

Her chest blazed but it was cold at the same time, felt as if someone had hollowed it out, had torn her heart from it and crushed it.

The tears that threatened lined his black lashes instead, pooled in his eyes like diamonds and slipped onto his cheeks, dashing down them to soak into her skin.

On a pained snarl that revealed sharp fangs, he tore away from her, stormed across the room and shoved the door to the outside open.

Isadora stared at where he had been, struggling to shut down the pain that crashed over her in powerful waves, a destructive force that utterly wrecked her.

Just as it had wrecked him.

She looked at the door he had exited through.

What was he to her?

What was she to him?

Would Apollyon be able to tell her?

Rook had mentioned taking her to Paris, which meant the rumours had been true and Apollyon was there. Apollyon had lured him to this world to find her. Rook was important to her, connected to her somehow. He had been able to locate her, and had been driven to save her, and to protect her.

She drifted to the door and watched him as he paced, taking swift agitated steps across the small clearing in front of the chalet that caused his wings to shift. The tips of his longest feathers brushed the ground with each powerful stride. He pivoted and stormed back the way he had come, every muscle on his formidable body tensed and bulging. Confusion and hurt etched his handsome face in dark lines, flattened his lips and had the black slashes of his eyebrows drawn low above shimmering turquoise eyes that held the barest hint of anger.

She didn't have the heart to disturb him, not when she moved her focus to him and could feel the pain and conflict inside him, feelings that ran as deep in him as they did in her.

She didn't understand either.

The reaction to touching him, to looking into his eyes and seeking an answer there, had been fierce and had stripped her strength from her in an instant, hurling her into a mass of dark emotions that felt familiar yet new to her. It had her head tied in knots, thoughts tangled together in a way that made it impossible to find the start of each one to tug and free them from the mess.

If she had to name the emotion that had seized her the hardest, she would call it grief.

Was that the emotion that had taken hold of Rook too?

Was there a reason it had filled them both?

She needed answers, and now she felt certain that only Apollyon could give them to her. She needed to meet with him, as soon as possible. She needed to know what Rook had been to her.

More importantly, she needed to know what she had been to him.

When the sky began to change colour through the dense canopy of the pines, her focus shifted there. She absorbed the burnished golds and pinks, savouring the way they relaxed her and seemed to lift the weight from her shoulders.

She focused on them as her mind turned back the clock, tracing through everything that had happened, all she could remember and the pieces that were missing. There were gaps. She could recall her youth, how reckless she had been. It was a family trait, and it was the reason she had made something, although she couldn't remember what that something was now.

A charm?

She had wanted to protect someone in her bloodline.

Rook tensed and her focus fell to him as he scanned their surroundings.

"It's the wind," she murmured absently and he didn't look at her.

He remained alert, scouring the forest for an enemy he wouldn't find, not unless he found deer and other small animals threatening.

She remembered something bad happening, but it was only a feeling. She couldn't recall why she had been so afraid and in so much pain. Was that forgotten time a source of the grief she had felt on gazing into Rook's eyes? Had he shared that pain with her?

"Rook." She waited for him to stop and look at her, but he didn't. "What do you remember?"

"I found you in the chateau and you knew me. You said my name, Isadora. You *knew* me." He whirled to face her, his face a dark mask as he narrowed his turquoise eyes on her. The flecks of gold and green in them brightened, turning his irises more emerald, speaking of the agitation she could sense in him. "I left... and when I returned for you... you had forgotten me. I... it pissed me off... when I saw you were hurt. It... snapped... something in me."

Because he felt the same instincts as she did despite her lost memories? She felt a powerful need to be close to him, to tend to his healing wounds and destroy the ones who had caused them. Not the tree that had broken their fall, but the witch who had cast a spell on him.

Thorns.

She knew the dark magic that had been responsible for the marks on his legs, the thick bands of reddened skin that snaked up them and the vicious puncture wounds that littered them.

"You said you took care of them." She checked the healing wounds. "You killed them?"

He nodded. "Three servants and two witches."

That wasn't right.

"Three witches and three servants," she corrected him, sure he had simply miscounted.

Frenchie, London Town and Country Estate had been at the chateau. Bitch and Spanish Inquisition had still been away somewhere.

Would they come for her?

She planned to be long gone by the time they returned and would cover her trail as best she could. Now that her magic was free again, she could easily do that.

He shook his head and took a step towards her. "There was a male outside. He wore a long coat and had cast the barrier. I killed him first. Then I came to you... and saw what had happened. I flew into the courtyard and killed a servant, and then another. I found the third servant inside, with the second witch, a male with a British accent."

"A posh one?" Mother Earth, she hoped it had been.

Another dreadful shake of his head. "Far from it. He told me your spell had backfired when you had been trying to forget and had tried to stop it."

"Why would I do that?" Was it possible she hadn't wanted to forget whatever the spell had been taking from her?

"I don't know," he bit out.

She looked at Rook, was instantly swept up in his eyes again as they shifted and swirled green.

A feeling struck her, had grief welling up again, as powerful as before.

She hadn't wanted to forget him.

"I wasn't trying to forget you, Rook. I'm sure of it. I was trying to forget something else and my memories of you were caught up in it."

"Like collateral damage?" He huffed. "That's reassuring. You need to learn how to do magic."

She deserved that. She remembered enough about last night to recall telling him he needed flying lessons. His mishap had sent them tumbling through a tree, and hers had stolen memories of him from her, ones he was annoyed about her losing as much as she was.

He wanted answers, and she could give him none.

"So what was I trying to forget?" She frowned at the broken deck of the cabin.

"The other spell?" His deep voice curled around her, offering comfort she stole as uncertainty filled her.

"Another spell?" She lifted her eyes to meet his again.

He held her gaze. "I think it made you immortal and the witches who took you wanted to know it."

So she had tried to make herself forget it.

She could understand why. Such a spell would have to be powerful, and dangerous. Immortality didn't come cheap. There was always a price to pay for bending the rules of the universe in such a way. While a witch could gain it, something else would have to lose it in order to maintain the balance.

"After you killed London Town, you came to me?" She weathered his questioning look. "They were cautious to keep their names from me. There was Frenchie, London Town and Country Estate left at the chateau. Who did you kill?"

His expression turned pensive, his lips compressing as his dark eyebrows dipped low, narrowing his now-bright-green eyes. "London Town inside the chateau... and the one outside... Frenchie."

"Shit," she muttered. "We have to leave."

Because she had charted all their powers and Country Estate was the strongest of the three who had been left to guard her, and the most determined to get whatever spell she had just forgotten out of her for his sister.

Rook tensed again.

Isadora went to say it was just the wind.

Ice spread down her spine as power washed over her, magic that crept through the trees like tendrils, seeking prey.

Her eyes leaped to meet Rook's.

"He found us."

# CHAPTER 11

Isadora gasped as Rook swept her up into his arms and kicked off. She clung to his shoulders, tightly gripping his muscles as he flew through the trees, his lips a thin line that spoke of the pain she could feel in him.

His wing wasn't fully healed yet.

The breastplate of his armour formed beneath her fingers and she adjusted her grip, clutching the straps that locked the two sides together over his shoulders. He held her closer as his wings faltered and she curled up in his arms, her eyes shooting to the tops of the trees below them. He pulled up before they collided with the pines, and she breathed a sigh of relief as they cleared the forest and reached the frozen lake.

That sigh died on her lips as her gaze hit a dark shape on the vast field of white.

Country Estate.

He stilled and lifted his head, revealing his face to her as the hood of his thick black coat fell back.

"Dive!" She yanked on Rook's breastplate as blue light burst from Country Estate's hands, twin orbs of magic shooting towards them.

Rook shifted her in his arms and dropped, pinning his wings back. Icy wind battered her, instantly freezing her as they rocketed towards the lake so fast she felt sick and wanted to hide against his neck, shutting the world out. Only she couldn't. She couldn't take her eyes off the witch below her as he launched two more blue orbs at her and Rook, spells meant to freeze them, slowing them so they would be vulnerable to attack. She was already frozen stiff as it was, her teeth close to chattering as the frigid air buffeted her.

She gasped as Rook suddenly pulled up, twirled in the air and beat his wings, narrowly avoiding the first blue orb. He grunted and growled as the second struck his injured wing and a scream tore from her throat as they plummeted towards the lake.

Rook twisted beneath her.

Intending to take the brunt of the blow when they hit the ice.

Isadora wasn't going to let that happen.

She chanted words, felt the power in each one as the spell built, and let the magic flow through her as she focused on the lake.

She pulled her right hand from Rook's shoulder, releasing her death grip on him, and cast it towards the sheet of thick ice coming at them fast.

A pale shockwave erupted from her palm, rolling across the land and blasting the trees with enough force to make them sway and shake the snow from their branches. The ice shattered, the sound tearing through the stillness of the evening like thunder, and water burst upwards, spraying towards them.

Rook hit the geyser and she focused on it, using the spell to hold him in the air and gently lower them both. The water bent, forming a wave that cast them onto the untouched ice and sent them skidding across it.

"Well, shit… that was…" He stared up at her as they slid to a halt, a twinkle in his blue-green eyes she liked, one that said he was impressed, and maybe a little proud of her.

"You can tell me how amazing I am later." She stilled as a sense of déjà vu ran through her, as if she had spoken those words to him before.

Country Estate caught her with a blast of power that sent her flying across the lake.

She hit the ice and skimmed across it, heading for the bank nearest the cabin.

"Isadora!" Rook started after her, furiously trying to fly despite his injured wing as he skidded around on the ice, in danger of losing his footing.

She opened her mouth to tell him to run.

A second blast struck his right wing, tearing a howl from his lips as he was spun around to face Country Estate, and she could only stare as blood sprayed across the white. She scrambled onto her feet, a spark igniting inside her as she pushed off and sprinted towards Rook.

Country Estate's dark eyes narrowed as he grinned, a flash of victory crossing his features that chilled her blood. The longer lengths of his fair hair and the tails of his black coat whipped in the wind that swirled like a vortex around him as magic sparked in his palms and his expression darkened.

Isadora pushed herself harder, the power she could feel building in the air driving her to reach Rook before it was too late. Her boots skidded on the ice, hindering her progress as she desperately tried to close the distance between her and the angel.

The witch hit him with another spell before she was even halfway to him, ripping a bellow from him that shook her to her core.

Had that spark becoming a wildfire in her blood.

Rook fell to his knees, shaking violently as he reached for his right wing and tried to move it. Blood dripped from his crimson feathers, a shade darker than them, and soaked into the snow covering the ice, forming a pool that rapidly spread outwards beneath him.

"Rook!" She reached for him, heart clenching and eyes widening as Country Estate suddenly appeared before him and grasped him by his neck.

Darkness flashed across the witch's face as he glared down at Rook. A memory surged almost to the surface of her mind before it shattered, leaving broken pieces of a moment she had definitely wanted to forget.

One where she had been in a terrible place that was darker than night, where something important had been stripped from her by creatures who wore that same look, hungered for violence and bloodshed as viciously as this witch did.

Country Estate's dark gaze slid to her and a knowing smile tilted his lips.

Rook growled, clamped his hand around the witch's wrist, and wiped the smile from his face as he shoved to his feet and flashed sharp red teeth.

Another memory flared in response, a clearer picture of the creatures who had hurt her, had stripped her strength from her piece by piece to break her all those centuries ago before they had destroyed her.

Darkness rolled over Rook's skin, snaking up from his wrists and his ankles to devour the bronzed warmth of it and leave it as black as midnight.

He snarled and his hand shot out and closed around Country Estate's neck. That snarl became a grin as he hauled the witch into the air, sending shock rippling across his face. It didn't last long. The witch rallied, grabbed Rook's arms just above his elbows and grinned right back at him.

Rook unleashed an unholy roar as his big body juddered. He threw his head back, the harrowing sound tearing through the falling night as he sank back to his knees on the ice and struggled to keep hold of the witch.

Isadora started running again, determined to reach him, to help him.

Country Estate yanked his left hand away from Rook's arm and pressed it into the ice.

"No!" She cast a teleportation spell, desperation flooding her as a circle of the thick ice beneath Rook disappeared.

She appeared just as Country Estate leaped clear of Rook and threw herself forwards, skidding across the ice to reach Rook as he plummeted into the frigid water.

Her hands hit the edge of the hole as he went under.

The ice reappeared.

"No... no... no!" She scrambled on her hands and knees, rubbing her palms over the ice, trying to see through it.

Rook banged against it from the other side.

Her heart clenched.

The wildfire became an inferno.

Her thoughts blurred, a cacophony she didn't hear as power surged through her and darkness consumed her, a black need to bloody her hands and destroy that she couldn't control.

No one was going to take him from her.

Not again.

She slammed her fists into the ice, shattering the area beneath her into tiny fragments that sprayed into the air all around her, and dropped into the icy dark abyss of the water. It instantly froze her skin, sapped the heat from her muscles and had her entire body cramping, but she wouldn't let it stop her. She swam downwards, kicking as hard as she could as her legs stiffened, following the beat that drummed inside her, one that grew stronger as she neared the faint power she could sense below her.

She fumbled in the darkness, fingers touching nothing, water rippling between them as she desperately searched.

Her hands hit something.

Solid. Warm.

Rook.

She grabbed him and kicked, pumping her legs and swimming in the direction she had come. She switched her focus to the trees, using them to guide her to the surface. Her lungs burned and she couldn't keep her mouth closed, gasped as she swallowed the vile water and it froze her from the inside too.

But it couldn't kill her.

She had tried drowning once.

Never again.

She breached the surface, spluttered and coughed as she purged the water from her burning lungs and struggled for air. She pulled Rook with her, tugging him towards a solid area of the ice as she shook violently, her body in danger of shutting down as the adrenaline that had surged through her, giving her the courage to go after Rook, flooded out of her.

She leaned against it when she reached it, clinging to it and to Rook as she tried to gather her strength. It leached from her, the cold stealing it together with fear. She glanced at Rook, terror gripping her in icy claws that pierced her heart as she saw how pale he was.

How still.

"Don't you die." She hauled herself onto the ice, rolled and pulled him with her, using a little of her power to assist her with his dead weight.

When he was out of the water, she collapsed next to him and feathered her trembling fingers over his throat, seeking a pulse.

She couldn't find one.

Isadora tore his breastplate off and pressed her ear to his chest.

Sighed and sank against him as a faint heartbeat thudded against it.

That relief washed from her as she grew aware of the witch on the other side of the lake.

One who had almost taken Rook from her.

She rose onto her feet and turned slowly to face him.

One who would pay for hurting him.

Darkness surged through her, power so strong it felt as if it was tearing her apart as it blazed in her veins, lit up her blood and stole command of her body again. She gave in to it, let it flow through her and fill her mind and heart, because she needed it.

Country Estate's hands began to glow crimson.

Isadora didn't give him a chance to attack.

She threw both hands forwards, her wrists touching as she thrust her palms towards him, and screamed as she unleashed every drop of her strength, every molecule of the writhing fury that boiled inside her.

A blast of violet blazed from her palms, shooting in a thick beam of lightning across the lake, stilted ribbons of it snapping at the ice as it rocketed towards the witch.

It exploded in a dazzling dome of white as it struck him and a smile slowly curled her lips as his scream rent the air and echoed around the mountains. The ice beneath her shook, trembling violently as she funnelled more of her strength into it, gave every piece of herself to the magic in the hope it would give her something in return.

Revenge.

The echoes of the scream faded and the beam stuttered, shrinking until it was only a thin faintly glowing line in the falling darkness and then nothing.

She breathed hard, every inch of her cold but on fire at the same time, her muscles liquid beneath her chilled skin and her bones on the verge of breaking.

"Isadora." A deep voice came from behind her, laced with pain that had a need to destroy welling up inside her again even when she was too weak to satisfy it.

She looked back over her shoulder at him.

Her beautiful angel.

Her one true love.

Magic chased around her wrists, faintly pulsing along lines invisible to her eyes, ribbons that tied her to him, entwined their souls and gave them one life, shared between them.

"Rook," she murmured, heat flooding her, joy that pushed the cold out and had her taking a step towards him so she could satisfy the ache to hold him and kiss him.

Pain erupted on her arms and she looked down.

Fire chased over the markings and bruises broke out on her pale skin, black and ugly, as her magic gained strength again and the spell she had foolishly cast drew on it, reinforcing itself.

Her eyes leaped to his.

"No."

She didn't want to forget him again.

Cold swept over her, stealing the last of her strength.

Darkness devoured her.

# CHAPTER 12

Rook caught Isadora as she fell, stopping her from hitting the fractured ice. A grimace tugged at his lips as pain ripped through his right wing and he dropped to his knees, landing with her in his lap.

He curled over her, clutching her to his bare chest, and breathed hard, trying to shut down the white-hot fire pulsing through his bones, ricocheting along the length of his wing and into his shoulder.

"Fuck," he muttered, his voice raw from screaming when the damned witch had come close to killing him.

He could still taste the water of the lake. It laced his tongue together with the tang of his own blood.

Next time he fought a witch, he wouldn't underestimate them. He would go all out from the start, regardless of the consequences.

He drew back and gazed down at Isadora, canting his head as he took in her ashen cheeks.

When she woke, would she remember what she had seen?

He had been close to going fully demonic and he was sure she had witnessed it, had seen the transformation coming over him.

Would she despise him? Fear him?

The thought had crossed his mind at the time, but he had pushed through the pain it had caused him, reaching for his other form because he had needed the strength it granted him.

He had needed the power to protect her.

He gently rubbed her cheek and then her arms, trying to get some warmth into her frigid skin. She was too pale, looking too close to death despite being apparently immortal. He curled his left wing around her and held her closer, attempting to warm her with his body despite the fact his wings were soaking wet and he was freezing, his limbs shaking violently as the cold sank deep into his bones. He needed to get her somewhere safe, and warm, where she could recover.

He slowly rose onto his feet, agony rolling through him as he straightened his tired legs and lifted Isadora in his arms. He struggled for breath, fought to shut down the pain and keep it under control, and trembled as he held her close to him.

He couldn't give in to the exhaustion washing through him. Not yet.

Isadora still wasn't safe.

He needed her safe.

He needed to protect her.

He gazed down at her again and how vulnerable she was struck him like a thunderbolt, had him holding her closer and aching to curl both of his wings around her.

Another feeling struck him too.

How good it felt to hold her.

When she had cuddled up to him last night in the cabin, seeking his warmth, he hadn't been sure what to do. In the end, he had sent his breastplate away and surprise had claimed him when she had snuggled closer to him, coming to press against his bare chest. Her delicate hands had scalded him as they had settled against his pectorals, and her scent had invaded his lungs, branding itself on his heart, a soft fragrance he found impossible to describe, but one that was the opposite of everything he breathed in Hell.

She was light. Flowers and sunshine. Blue skies and the infinite ocean. She was nature in its most beautiful form.

Hell was nature in its ugliest incarnation.

He could see that now he had met her.

He lowered his head and breathed her in, the scent of her surprising him once again as it seemed to restore some of his strength, gave him back a sliver of it, enough that he could move with her.

He walked towards the edge of the ice and his black heart ached when she gave him a sweet sign of life by shifting closer to him, seeking his warmth.

Rook had been greedy last night when she had sought his heat, and he was just as greedy now. He eagerly used the excuse of warming her to hold her closer still, to encourage her to burrow her face against the crook of his neck. Her warm breath skated across his skin, sending a sharp thrill through him that had his blood heating so fast he no longer noticed the cold.

Every inch of him heated in response to the feel of her, how she pressed against him and how good she smelled.

He lowered his head as they reached the shore of the lake and hesitated for only a heartbeat before he brushed his lips across her forehead. She tilted her head up, a little sigh escaping her.

"Rook," she husked, her voice barely there.

"I'm here." Where he would always be.

Where he was meant to be.

He felt that deep in his bones, in the pit of his soul, as he gazed down at her again.

This was where he belonged.

And that terrified him.

What if the reason the Devil wasn't calling him back was because he was right where his master wanted him to be?

She had said angels like him had taken her before.

He cast that thought aside. He wouldn't take her to Hell. He wouldn't do it. His master could use the most powerful compulsion at his disposal on him and he wouldn't do it. She had been through enough.

He couldn't cast his next thought aside so easily.

Why had the Devil wanted her?

Whatever the reason, he couldn't have her.

He was weak right now, but he would protect her.

He gently set her feet down on the snow, kept her tucked close to him with his right arm and held his left one out before him. The air shimmered a metre in front of him, causing the trees in the distance to ripple violently as the portal built. A dark spot formed in the centre and spread outwards, threads of it chasing through the swirling air to devour it. When the oval was as tall as he was, the oily black burst into white flames and a glow lit the night, throwing the shadows out long all around him.

He looked down at Isadora to check she was still out cold, because while a part of him was aware she had already witnessed what he was, the rest held on to hope that she didn't know. He didn't want her to see the portal. He didn't want her to discover he was a Hell's angel. Foolish dreams that would never come true.

It was too late to try to hide it from her.

Although, there was a chance the forgetting spell that had come back with a vengeance to bruise her fair skin and tear a pained cry from her ashen lips would steal the memory from her.

Would she remember what she had seen when he had been fighting the witch?

Would she remember him?

He had seen the flicker of recognition in her eyes after she had turned the witch into a smouldering black streak on the ice. She had known him. Really known him. Not just the Rook she had known since he had rescued her, but the one she had known before. The Rook he couldn't remember.

But then those bruises had formed and panic had crossed her delicate features, and she had collapsed.

Damn, he wanted her to remember him, even when he knew she wouldn't.

She stirred again and he smoothed another kiss across her damp brow. She calmed and pride welled up again, causing a flicker of light in his black heart, one that made him want to kiss her again just so he could absorb the way she reacted, how she relaxed and sought more, tried to lift herself to press against his lips.

He strode towards the portal, aware he was going to have to swallow a lot of that pride when he hit the other side.

Paris.

As much as he hated the idea of turning to an angel for help, he had to go through with it. If there was even the smallest of chances that Apollyon's witch could help Isadora, he would take it. He would do whatever he had to in order to make sure Isadora received the care she needed.

Because there was nothing he could do for her.

In his current condition, he couldn't even protect her.

He was useless to her until he healed, and even then he wasn't sure he could keep her safe, not if his suspicions were correct and his master wanted him here with her for some reason.

Rook stepped out of the portal onto the roof of a large pale stone building in the centre of the city. It was quiet around him, the elegant streets empty save a few vehicles moving along them. Clouds hung heavily in the air, glowing orange from the city lights, and the scent of snow laced the night.

He held Isadora closer as she trembled in his arms and wrapped his wings around her as best he could. When fire blazed through his right one, he gave up trying to move it and settled for having his left one around her, keeping her warm.

He stared at the twinkling city that stretched around him. Waiting. Feeling even more useless.

Hell's angels couldn't communicate telepathically with angels of Heaven.

He had come to Paris, but he had no clue where Apollyon lived, was banking on the angel feeling his presence and finding him.

"Hang on, Isadora," he murmured and brushed another kiss across her brow when she moaned and curled closer to him.

It was a risk, but he had to take it.

He kept his eyes on her as he called on his demonic form, willing her to remain asleep because he was sure she would freak the fuck out if she woke to find herself in the arms of a Hell's angel.

He had to do it though.

His demonic form would send a stronger signal across the city, one Apollyon was more likely to notice.

Although, any other angel in the city would feel his presence too.

He gritted his teeth as his wings transformed, the crimson running from them to leave black feathers, and grunted as those feathers fell to reveal the leathery membrane beneath. His vision wavered, the fire that rolled through him so intense he struggled to breathe through it.

The hands that gently cradled Isadora turned as black as basalt as he grew in size and his eyesight sharpened as his irises shifted to scarlet.

He expected the switch to his demonic form to alter him in different ways, to harden his heart and turn it cold, but as he gazed down at Isadora where she rested against his blackened skin, he felt only warmth and hope.

The king of fools.

She could never love him.

A flash of the way she had looked at him on the lake before she had passed out overlaid onto her.

Although, maybe she already loved him.

Or at least she had loved the angel he had once been.

"Rook." The deep male voice startled him from his reverie and he growled at the intruder, flashing all-sharp red teeth. Apollyon landed, his black wings furling against his back, and held his hands up. "I apologise."

Rook held his ground as the angel advanced, but tucked Isadora closer to his chest, unable to deny the need to protect her from the male.

Because he didn't want the angel to take her from him.

Because he was falling for her.

Or maybe he was just remembering that he loved her.

He glanced down at her, and lingered, unable to tear his gaze away from her.

"Is that Isadora?" Apollyon moved another step closer and canted his head to his left, causing his long black ponytail to sway that way as he tried to peer past Rook's leathery wing.

Rook nodded.

"I found her. She remembered me... but then she forgot. I think it's a spell." He couldn't stop the words from spilling from him as he looked at her, as he dared to hope again that somehow she would remember him and would look at him with that glimmer of affection in her eyes again. "She remembered me again after she had fought a witch and killed him."

"Some sort of magical exhaustion," Apollyon muttered and studied her as Rook moved his wing, allowing the angel a glimpse at her. "Serenity has studied such things. How a spell can be affected when the witch is weakened and how it reacts when the witch regains their strength."

Isadora had truly remembered him then. In that moment, when she had looked at him with so much love in her eyes, she had known him.

"Hell's angels took her before." The words slipped from his lips and when he glanced at Apollyon, the male didn't appear surprised to hear it.

"I know. I am sorry, Rook, perhaps I should have told you before… but I needed to give you a reason to find her, and the truth wasn't it." The look in Apollyon's blue eyes backed up that apology, so while it was tempting to bust the angel's balls over the fact he had been holding out on him, he let it go.

There were far more important things he needed to do. Taking care of Isadora ranked the highest, but now that Apollyon was with him again, questions were forming in Rook's mind and they wouldn't be ignored.

"The truth? You said I was a guardian angel once… her guardian angel." He dropped his gaze to her again as the pieces fell into place. "I followed her there, didn't I?"

"You did. You went to save her."

"And I failed… or did I succeed?" He brushed his fingers along her arm where he held it.

She had survived, had escaped the realm he now called home, and she had lived, at least a thousand years, because he had been in the service of the Devil for that long.

"I thought she was dead," Apollyon said, drawing his focus back to him. "I thought you were dead. But then I saw you again, a long time ago, and I knew something terrible had happened."

Because he had fallen.

Because of her?

He didn't remember her. Was that a spell? Had she made him forget her, or had someone else?

No, it hadn't been her. She had been shocked to see him, and she had remembered him. He had witnessed the pain, the grief that had filled her eyes, and the relief. Apollyon wasn't the only one who had thought him dead. She had too.

So who had taken his memories of her from him?

His gut gave him the answer to that question, but it didn't give him the reason.

His master.

The Devil had the power to manipulate those in his service. It was possible the male had made him forget his past life, one he should have recalled as the other Hell's angels did. Why? What purpose had it served?

Another piece of the puzzle slipped into place.

Isadora knew a spell that had made her immortal.

He looked at his hands, focusing not on them but on his wrists and the ink his vambraces concealed, and the answer to their origin and meaning hit him hard.

She had made them. It had been her voice in his mind, promising him forever, when the marks had burned back in Hell.

She was bound to him.

# CHAPTER 13

Isadora woke to the sensation of being watched. Not in a bad, creepy sort of way, but in a way that left her feeling protected. She lifted her hand, rubbed sleep from her eyes, and slowly opened them. She settled them on the black-haired warrior sat on a white wooden chair beside her bed.

His wings were gone, and so was his armour. Black jeans rode low on his hips and a t-shirt stretched tight over his broad chest, hugging his muscles in a way that looked as if someone had painted him obsidian. There were black leather cuffs covering his forearms from wrist to close to his elbow.

She saw a flash of darkness crawling over his golden skin, covering it.

Of crimson feathers falling away to reveal dragon-like wings.

He wasn't an angel of Heaven.

But as she looked at him, his origins didn't matter to her. He was the same handsome, gruff, and protective angel who had rescued her from the witches, had avenged her and taken care of her.

And had brought her to what appeared to be a rather expensive apartment somewhere.

Paris?

She recalled him mentioning wanting to take her back to that city.

"You're awake." His deep voice was low, a little rough, and her stomach somersaulted as another memory assaulted her.

One where he had been sinking into the black abyss of the lake.

A chill swept down her spine and she sat bolt upright, a desperate need to be close to him, to touch him and feel he was with her rushing through her.

"You shouldn't move." He rose from his seat, came to the bed and sat beside her.

A flicker of something crossed his stunning turquoise eyes, an emotion that resembled fear. Nerves? The reason for it became clear when he lifted his hand and carefully brushed her silver hair from her face, clearing it from her cheeks and hooking it behind her ears. His touch was light and sent a shiver through her, a pleasant sort of heat that had her wanting to lean into his tender caress.

"You had me worried there for a moment." He gave her a tight smile.

"How long was I out?" She looked at her surroundings again. "And where are we?"

"We're in Paris… with… friends. At least, you might remember him." He glanced over his shoulder at the door set into the white wall beyond the foot of the bed and sighed. "The witch who lives here has been taking care of you. She did something to funnel magic back into you or some shit like it… and now I have to tell her she was right about you recovering and waking today."

Which upset him for some reason. Because he hadn't been able to do that for her? Had he wanted to be the one to bring her back from whatever dark place she had been in?

She remembered being furious when he had been hurt. She remembered unleashing all of that rage on Country Estate.

And then she remembered… something.

She couldn't put her finger on it.

Whenever she tried, her head ached and faint pain bloomed in her bones.

"Don't." Rook shook his head and captured both of her cheeks in his warm palms. She let go of trying to remember and fell into his eyes, lost herself in them a little as he looked at her as if she was causing him pain by hurting herself. "The witch says she can help you with the spell you cast… so you can remember."

Mother Earth, she wanted that.

She schooled her features so he didn't see how badly she wanted the spell broken because the way he refused to call the witch who lived in the apartment by name told her something.

He didn't like the female.

Because this witch could help her and he couldn't?

A petite blonde bustled into the room and Rook's expression darkened as he eased back, confirming Isadora's suspicion.

"I felt you wake." The words held a French lilt.

A shadow loomed in the doorway beyond her and Isadora's eyes shifted there and widened as she recognised the dark angel.

"Apollyon." The name burst from her lips on a smile, one filled with all the relief she felt as she saw a familiar face, the very one she had hoped to see when she had come to the city.

Rook grumbled something and stood, and cold arrowed through her as he moved away, distancing himself.

She wanted to ask him to come back to her, but the witch and Apollyon moved to the spot he had been, blocking her view of him and stealing her focus.

"I thought if I funnelled some of my power into you that you would recover." The witch kneeled on the bed beside her and shook her head. "Where are my manners? I'm Serenity."

Isadora took the hand she offered and froze as they made contact, a sensation rolling through her that had her eyes leaping to meet Serenity's hazel ones.

Serenity smiled softly. "I felt it too, when I was helping you. We are of the same blood."

The comfort Isadora had felt on realising that gave way to panic and she gripped the blonde's hand, holding it tightly so Serenity couldn't pull away. "Be careful. There are forces at work that are a danger to our bloodline."

Serenity nodded, her expression turning grave as she looked between her eyes and her wrists. "Is it the reason you cast a spell on yourself?"

Isadora shook her head. "No. I don't think so."

"I told you. She did it to protect a spell." Rook's deep growl reeked of the irritation she could feel in him and she ached to have him move so she could see him.

He was annoyingly determined to distance himself though.

Well, he could try to pull away from her all he wanted. She wasn't going to let it happen.

She released Serenity, pushed the bedclothes aside, and slipped from the bed, not caring that she wore only her underwear and a long black t-shirt that was five sizes too big for her. She hazarded a guess that it belonged to Rook. Or at least, she hoped it did.

She ignored Serenity as the woman tried to stop her and walked on unsteady legs around the bed.

The moment Rook noticed she had moved, he was in front of her.

"Holy fucking hell, Isadora." He glared off to his right, toward Apollyon, and growled, "You're not dressed."

"I'm as dressed as I need to be." She placed her hands against his chest and his heart thudded against her palms, a strong rapid beat that spoke of anger.

Anger that wasn't directed at her.

It was directed at Apollyon.

Because she was 'not dressed' in front of another male?

The t-shirt reached her thighs, covering everything but her legs. She wasn't flashing anything at Apollyon, but Rook reacted like she was naked, and that told her something that warmed her heart and brought a smile to her lips.

Rook liked her.

He couldn't remember her, just as she couldn't remember him, but he was still attracted to her.

Just as she was attracted to him.

Heat burned in his eyes as they came back to rest on her and a faint ring of crimson encircled his dilating pupils, glowing brighter the longer he looked at her. As it fully emerged, he turned his cheek to her and lowered his gaze.

She frowned, cupped his cheek with her right hand and tried to make him look at her again.

He locked up tight, making it impossible, and she sighed as it hit her that he didn't want her to see the scarlet in his eyes. He was afraid of it happening.

"I'm not scared of you, Rook," she whispered, tiptoed and pressed a soft kiss to his cheek. She breathed against it, "So stop thinking I am... or I ever could be."

His gaze slid towards her, his irises a strange blend of turquoise to scarlet. "You remembered."

She nodded. "And now I want to remember you."

She focused on her body and conjured a knee-length black dress that hugged her curves.

Rook's eyes dropped to it and the way they darkened made her feel she was wearing even less than she had been a moment ago, not more. That familiar heat built in them, and damn she wanted to act on it this time, was wound tight with a need to touch him and lose herself in him, to know him fully at last and know he was with her, safe and unharmed.

Those urges and desires were confusing as much as they were consuming.

Her mind couldn't recall him, but she felt connected to him, drawn to him and unable to breathe when she was close to him like this. The way he crowded her with his big body, the way his gaze hungrily raked over her, and the heat of him had her wanting to step into him, to press against him and tempt him into surrendering to the need that flared in his eyes.

Need that echoed inside her.

She forced herself to break contact with him and peered past him instead. "Serenity?"

The blonde nodded. "I can lift the spell. I will need to concentrate though."

Serenity shot a look at Apollyon and Rook, her hazel eyes silently conveying her desire for them to leave.

Apollyon left without hesitation. Rook lingered, his eyes locked on her, concern written in their blue-green depths.

Isadora smiled slightly. "I'll be fine."

He still didn't move.

She cupped his cheeks, tilted his head down towards her, and stared up into his eyes as she swept her thumbs along his cheekbones.

She didn't want him to go either, but Serenity needed quiet to perform the spell. It would be complicated and dangerous. Even the slightest slip in concentration could prove disastrous.

Isadora really didn't need another spell going haywire inside her.

"I'll call you if I need you, Rook," she whispered and stroked his cheeks.

His eyes darkened, turning stormy, and then he huffed and tossed a glare at Serenity. "I'll be right outside."

He broke away from her. She watched him go and wasn't surprised when he planted his fine ass against the wall on the other side of the open door, folded his arms across his chest and leaned back against it.

Serenity muttered in French, "And I thought Apollyon could be moody and protective."

Isadora smiled at that and couldn't stop her eyes from wandering over Rook. She liked it. He wasn't protective in an overbearing way, one that belittled her strength and left her feeling as if she was feeble and couldn't take care of herself.

He was protective in a way that made her feel stronger, supported by him, as if no matter what happened, he would always be in her corner. He would always be there for her, to help her if she needed it, to do whatever she asked of him, whatever she desired. He had her back.

It left her feeling as if they were a team.

As if she was no longer alone.

Her chest tightened at that, heart aching at the thought the long cold centuries she had endured might have finally come to an end and that from now on, she might never be alone again.

She could have Rook walking beside her through life if she could convince him they were meant to be.

It was odd feeling such a way when her mind said she had only known him a few days.

Her heart whispered she had known him forever.

"Mother Earth, get rid of this damned spell." She turned to Serenity, a smile wobbling on her lips. "I want to remember him again."

She couldn't take her instincts and her mind warring anymore. She knew Rook. He was more than just a relative stranger to her. Her mind could offer blank patches all it wanted when she tried to remember him, because her heart filled them in, grew warm and light whenever she encountered a gap in her memories, and she knew it was because of him.

Because she loved him.

That love had transcended the boundaries of the spell. It had broken through it despite the spell's attempts to strip her of her feelings as well as her memories.

It was a struggle to focus as Serenity approached her and took hold of her hands. She closed her eyes and drew down a slow breath as Serenity's power flowed over her skin and didn't resist it as it met her own magic. She answered all of Serenity's questions about the spell she might have used, telling her which ones she had at her disposal, and tried to be patient as the petite blonde worked her way through counter spells.

A shadow moved across her mind, sending a shiver over her skin, and she snapped her eyes open.

"You're close." She could feel the spell she had cast being drawn to the surface, and could feel it as it resisted the words Serenity chanted in a low voice as she gripped her wrists.

Isadora twisted her arms so she could clamp her hands around Serenity's wrists and form a stronger connection between them. As the spell surfaced, she locked onto it just as fiercely.

"It's Melchizedek's Fifth Incantation of Order." She conjured the reversal spell in her mind as Serenity nodded and tightened her grip on Isadora's wrists.

They chanted it together and her eyes slid to half-mast as power built between them, swirled and grew stronger, causing the fine tips of her silver hair to float and dance.

She felt eyes on her, hot and searing, and glanced at Rook. Her gaze locked with his as he looked over his shoulder at her and a sudden crush of emotions threatened to take her legs out from under her as they turned liquid, all of her strength flooding from her in response to the memories stirring back to life inside her.

Centuries of mourning him, yearning for the chance to see him again, aching to touch him and hear his voice lightening the darkness in her heart swept over her, stealing her voice so Serenity had to continue alone. Tears filled her eyes as she looked at him, as memories of the time that had come before the long dark days without him resurfaced, warming her heart.

Mother Earth, she loved that man who was looking at her with a wealth of concern in his eyes, in a way that said he wanted to come to her and comfort her, but didn't want to ruin what was happening by intruding.

He needed to come to her.

Damn, she needed to go to him too.

She needed to hold him in her arms and feel his around her. She needed to know he was alive and he was finally back with her. She needed him, more now than ever, wasn't sure she could breathe until she was being held by him, was breathing him in and soaking up his warmth.

The flood of memories continued, darker ones surfacing that tore at her aching heart and had her lost in thoughts of how she was going to tell him everything that had happened to him, and to her. He needed to know. His memories were locked away, but she could tell him things about himself, could help fill in the blanks so he could know what they had been to each other once.

And what she wanted to be to him again.

She was so swept up in the need to go to him and tell him everything that she didn't notice what Serenity was doing until it was almost too late.

Her wrists burned.

Isadora snatched her hands back. "Don't!"

Her chest seized as she looked down at her wrists, afraid she would be able to see the spell inscribed on them. Relief stole another piece of her strength from her as she saw only pale skin and fading bruises, and felt the spell was intact, still hiding the markings from everyone.

"What's wrong?" Rook barged into the room, darkness spreading outwards from around his crimson eyes as he glared at Serenity and then looked at her.

Isadora shook her head. "It's nothing… just… she almost broke the spell."

"The one that makes you forget me?" His expression softened and the tension drained from his broad shoulders as the darkness around his eyes lifted. "You mean the spell that protects the one you cast between us."

Her eyes widened and heat burned her cheeks, scalding them with the intensity of a thousand suns. "You know?"

He nodded. "I figured it out. You're immortal because you're bound to me… you want to protect the spell from people because you want to protect other immortals from witches who might abuse it."

Her gaze fell to his forearms as he removed the black leather cuffs that protected them.

"It looks like this, right?" He held his hands out to her, revealing beautiful intricate bands of markings that encircled his forearms.

She was the one who nodded this time, relief sweeping through her at the thought it was one less thing she had to find a way to explain to him.

When he looked at her wrists, she knew what he wanted.

She pulled down a steadying breath and focused on them as she held them out towards him. She whispered words that would temporarily lift the spell that concealed them. It was dangerous because it wouldn't only allow everyone to see the markings. Witches would be able to sense it if they were looking for the spell's unique marker in the flow of magic around the world.

She had to do it though.

She had to show Rook that she bore the same markings as him, that he wasn't alone in this world, and neither was she. They had each other.

He moved towards her and she didn't stop him when he skimmed his fingers over the swirls and lines that matched his. He frowned as they faded, sinking back into her skin.

"I can't let them out for long." She wished that she could, because she had been enjoying the feel of his hands on her, his light caress that had heat rolling through her veins again.

"You hid them to protect Rook. You were afraid someone would recognise you had bound yourself to a powerful being and they would use it against you." Apollyon appeared in the doorway, his blue eyes narrowed beneath the tightly knit black slashes of his eyebrows as he looked at her wrists. "Or you feared someone would use you against him."

"It's more than that." She looked from Rook to him. "Rook is right, and I don't want it being used by witches to bind an immortal to them against their will. Magic is a balance. To make me immortal, it has tied my life to Rook's, but it has also affected him."

"How?" Rook frowned down at her.

"I'm not sure…" She tried to hold his gaze but her courage faltered as his frown deepened. "I'm not sure what might happen if you did die. I'm not sure you would be reborn. You said you didn't care… that one life with me was enough for you."

The darkness that had been filling his eyes faded away, and her heart went out to him when she felt his need to remember the memories he had lost and how it was a source of pain for him.

Pain she could ease.

She took hold of his wrists and focused on them.

Rook pulled free of her grip and gruffly muttered, "It's fine… let it go. I need some air."

He walked away before she could stop him, pushing past Apollyon and disappearing from view. Her gaze shifted to the other angel, one who had always been open with her, kind and a friend.

Apollyon sighed. "Rook believes the Devil took his memories for some reason."

It was possible. The Devil had known Rook was bound to her and it was like that devious creature to do whatever it took to keep hold of something that could prove valuable to him, even robbing someone of their precious memories.

Her stomach tightened and swirled as she thought about that, as her mind conjured the reason Rook had been stripped of his past.

It was her fault.

She had managed to escape Hell and had gone into hiding, grief-stricken and convinced Rook was dead. The Devil had somehow made Rook fall and had taken his memories to keep Rook under his sway, had made Rook serve him waiting for the day that she resurfaced and he could send Rook after her.

Because he wanted the talisman.

He would never find it. She would never tell him. History could repeat itself and she would endure it all over again. The talisman she had created to protect the bearer of it was too important for her to break, even more important than keeping the spell that bound her to Rook out of the hands of witches.

Besides, she didn't know where the talisman was now.

She glanced at Serenity.

She didn't want to know.

Serenity was of her blood and could tell her, which meant she had to get away from the young witch as soon as possible.

Which meant convincing Rook to leave with her.

# CHAPTER 14

Isadora found Rook on a small terracotta-tiled terrace, early evening light casting golden highlights in the tangled strands of his short dark hair. It caressed his shoulders too, accenting muscles that were tense beneath his black t-shirt as he braced his hands against the wrought iron railing opposite the door.

She moved to stand beside him, keeping only a small distance between them, and mirrored his stance, taking hold of the railing and gazing up at the sky above the elegant townhouses opposite her.

"I… I'm sorry for everything that happened to you." There, it was out there now, no longer burning inside her, destroying her from the inside.

The guilt she felt didn't lessen. It only grew more intense as his head swivelled towards her and his eyes landed on her.

"It wasn't your fault." His deep voice curled around her, offering comfort she refused to take, because he didn't know what he was talking about, wouldn't say such a thing if he remembered what had happened.

"It was." She kept her eyes on the sky as it changed colour, the threads of cloud that laced it making the sunset beautiful, but her focus was on the man beside her, one who deserved a thousand apologies from her.

He deserved to know the truth too.

She breathed slowly to steady her racing heart as nerves began to get the better of her and pushed herself to continue, to let it all spill out of her, not only so he would know about the life he couldn't remember, but so she could lift some of the burden from her own shoulders.

She had been waiting more than a thousand years to tell him she had been a fool, had ruined something wonderful because she had been headstrong and reckless, and hadn't listened to him.

She had been waiting centuries for his forgiveness.

"You were against me going, so I slipped out in the night when you were sleeping. I went to meet with someone who said they could get me the ingredients I needed to make the talisman stronger, as close to perfect as it could be." She tightened her grip on the metal railing and lowered her head as guilt churned her stomach again. "You were right to be worried though… the 'people' had turned out to be demonic angels."

"When you were out of it after the forgetting spell backfired, you talked about demons taking you." He twisted to face her and leaned a hip against the railing, trusting it far more than she could.

She supposed if he fell, he had wings to stop himself from hitting the ground.

She glanced at his back.

"Are they better now?" She jerked her chin towards his chest when he frowned, confusion dancing in his eyes. "Your wings."

He shifted his shoulders. "All fine now. Fit for flying again."

She was glad to hear that.

She inched closer to him, a little shuffle of her right foot she hoped he didn't notice. The need to be near him was strong, born of the fact she was afraid he would be angry with her when he learned the truth and she didn't want him to leave. She needed him close to her.

"The demonic angels took me to Hell." She tried to shut out the vision of that grim and terrible realm that invaded her mind, the memories of searing fiery rivers, choking thick air and screams that rang in the air.

Mother Earth, those shrieks and cries had never stopped. They had been constant, tearing at her, keeping her on the edge. Sometimes, they had been her screams.

The worst times, they had been Rook's.

She closed her eyes, needing to push that memory aside before it tore down her strength and stole her voice.

Rook's hand came to rest gently on her shoulder.

Isadora leaned her head towards it, raising her shoulder at the same time, a need to press against him and steal comfort from the feel of him filling her. He didn't take it away as her cheek pressed against his knuckles, kept it there for her and she was thankful for it. She needed his strength right now.

"The Devil came to see me more than once... demanded I told him where the talisman was and who I had made it for. Whenever I refused, he..." Her throat closed.

"Tortured you," Rook said for her and she nodded, shifting her cheek against his hand. He turned it and cupped her face. She lifted her eyes to his as he brushed his thumb across her cheek, his expression soft and filled with understanding. "I know the things he does."

She didn't want to ask whether he knew because he had been present, because he had been one of the angels who had done the Devil's bidding in his vile prison, tormenting those he held captive. She didn't need to ask. It was there in his eyes, laced with a flicker of a guilt she found surprising given what he was now, but also unsurprising at the same time because he was still Rook.

Whatever the Devil had done to him, however that wretch had shaped him, he was still Rook deep inside him, where it mattered most.

The heart that beat in his chest, the soul that was bound to hers, was the same as it had always been.

"You found me," she whispered, the thought of what she had to tell him next trying to steal the voice she had just found. "They... hurt you to get to me... did horrible things to you in front of me... but you refused to give in, and so I refused too. I drew from your strength... your unwavering belief in my need to protect the one I had made the talisman for, because it had been a great strain on me to create it... it had almost killed me."

She shook her head when he looked as if he wanted to speak and edged closer to him, until she could feel his heat and smell his rich masculine scent more clearly, and the fear that was building in her ebbed away again.

"The Devil was furious. He raged so violently all of Hell was shaken by it and so was I. I was terrified... but you... you were unmoved, calm despite the storm surrounding you." Tears lined her lashes as she remembered how he had knelt before her, blood streaming from the deep lacerations that covered his bare body, his wings distorted and broken, stained crimson and black, and how he had looked at her, his gaze unwavering, steady and filled with love, with courage that had bolstered her own, until what had happened next. "He moved me to another room. I tried to stay with you, but I wasn't strong enough to fight the men who held me. They hurt me... and I couldn't hold back the screams. Whenever I screamed, they hurt you to make you do the same."

His lips flattened and darkness crossed his features, bringing out that ring of crimson in his irises. His anger flowed into her through the point where he touched her, where his thumb kept up the light caress that soothed her, offering her comfort she badly needed as she thought about what they had done, and tried to piece together the truth for both of them.

"He brought in witches. I remember feeling power not born of Hell, but I was so out of it. The pain... it was... it was too much and I found it hard to focus. I was so tired." She frowned as she struggled to recall what she had felt then and make sense of it. "Our connection... it shattered and I thought you... I thought... you were... dead."

His expression sobered, but the flicker of fury in his eyes remained. "Now what do you think happened?"

What did she think?

She searched his eyes, seeing his need to know in them, how deeply he wanted to understand how he had come to fall.

She raised her hands and wrapped them both around the wrist of the one he held her face with and focused on it. "Now I think he used the witch to make us both believe the other was dead."

Grief had consumed her, pain that had blinded her to everything other than escaping, running from the hurt and somehow surviving until she was strong enough to either avenge Rook, or meet him again in his next life.

"He wanted me to suffer for refusing him, and I'm sure he thought it would break me." Her eyebrows knitted as she battled to remember what had happened.

It had been a blur.

Like when Rook had fallen through the ice and she had almost lost him.

"I was… there's darkness in me… in all of my bloodline. It took control of me and he couldn't contain me. I… think I might have destroyed half a cellblock before escaping."

Rook's right eyebrow lifted and a teasing smile curled his firm lips, one that removed some of the sombreness from the air and gave her relief. "There is a part of the western wing missing. I always wondered what happened to it. Figured the Devil had lost his temper… not a little witch."

Heat tried to creep onto her cheeks at that, but she tamped it down. "My family have a history of destruction."

It ran deep in their blood.

"So you escaped, and I fell." He tipped his head up and looked at the sky, his gaze distant as it traversed the gold-edged clouds.

Pain beat inside him and it flowed into her as she brushed her fingers over the markings on his forearm, wanting to draw his focus away from what had happened to him and back to her.

"I can help you remember, Rook."

His turquoise eyes slowly drifted back down to her.

She focused on his markings and then beyond them, funnelled her magic into his veins and muscles, seeking the other spell, the one she had sensed in the bedroom before he had pulled away from her and left her in search of some air.

"I think a witch might be responsible for what happened to you." She kept her focus on his body as the full weight of his attention came to rest on her, his eyes gaining a curious edge as they locked on her face. "I can feel dark magic in you… buried deep… so deep I'm not sure I can draw it to the surface to decipher what spell was cast on you… but I want to help you."

He lifted his free hand and cupped her other cheek with it, framing her face, and looked deep into her eyes. "While I would like to remember our time together... I don't care that I can't remember... hell, I might even say I prefer it this way... because I don't have to remember the pain like you do. I don't have to remember you dying... the thought that you had died."

She released his wrist and held his hands, keeping them on her face as her heart bled for him at the same time as it filled with warmth, stirred by the way he was looking at her with so much affection in his eyes and by the honesty in his words.

"I'm sorry," she whispered, needing to say it again.

He smiled tightly. "It isn't your fault. What happened... it was a long time ago, Isadora... and even if I could remember it, I would never hold it against you. If you need my forgiveness... then you have it. I don't think I could ever blame you for anything or hold a grudge against you for longer than a minute."

His smile warmed, lighting his eyes, an echo of the way he had looked at her a thousand times in the past when he had been far less serious and far more trouble.

He swept his thumbs across her cheeks, sending warmth skittering over her skin and lightening her insides as feelings stirred inside her, need she was no longer strong enough to deny.

"I'm happy with those memories gone," he husked, his eyebrows furrowing as he held her gaze. "I'm happy to make new ones with you."

He glanced at his wrists.

"A spell might hold my memories at bay, but the one you cast to bind us together still exists and it rises to the surface from time to time." His eyes fell back to the intricate swirls of the spell inscribed on him and softened. "When it happens... I'm drawn to staring at them, spend as long as it lasts studying them... mesmerised by them and struck by a sense they're important... more than just fancy ink."

His gaze shifted back to lock with hers.

"I don't need memories to make me feel something for you."

He dipped his head.

Claimed her lips in a kiss so soft it brought tears to her eyes.

Whispered against them.

"Isadora... I still love you."

# CHAPTER 15

Rook wasn't prepared for the sensations that detonated inside him as Isadora wrapped her arms around his neck and kissed him.

Softer emotions he had never experienced before ran rampant through him, swirled and entwined with the force of need that rose inside him, a hunger that compelled him to take more from her, to not release her until it was satisfied.

A groan slipped from his lips as she angled her head and deepened the kiss, and damn, it rocked him to his core.

Spilling the contents of his heart, admitting to soft feelings that had no place in his world, had been difficult, but hell, it had been worth it to see the way her aqua eyes had lit up and warmed as he confessed that he felt connected to her.

That he loved her.

She moaned, the sound sweet music to his ears as he held her closer, banded his arms around her back and lifted her. Another little sigh escaped her as he clutched her backside, and his own groan joined it as he palmed her. Holy hell, she felt good beneath his fingers, pressed against him. His already rock hard cock ached, throbbed with need that had a grimace pulling at his lips as he kissed her.

Nerves rose again, but he tamped them down, refused to acknowledge them and let them ruin this moment. Whatever happened, he could handle it.

The voice at the back of his mind taunted him, whispered that he couldn't. He had never been with a woman in his current life.

But that was wrong, wasn't it?

He had been with Isadora.

She destroyed his ability to think as she wrapped her long legs around his hips, her knees scalding him through his jeans.

"Rook," she husked as she devoured his mouth with kisses that were growing rougher, wilder, and damn, he could get in on some of that mindless passion where only feeling existed.

It was better than panicking that whatever happened between them, his lack of a memory was going to make it less than it should be. He wasn't inexperienced. He chanted that in his head as he kissed her, nipped at her lower lip with his blunt teeth and ripped another sultry moan from her. She rocked her hips forwards and he hissed through those teeth as her heat met his aching length.

"Need you." Those words, uttered in her sweet voice in a desperate way, were his undoing.

He growled, the need to satisfy her, to bring her to a shattering release that would ease her need of him and bring them closer together, rolling through him with the force of a tornado, leaving him wrecked.

She kissed him harder, her lips clashing with his, as he turned with her and carried her back into the apartment.

She didn't stop when Apollyon glanced at them from the living room, kept kissing him and working her body against his, driving him wild. Her lips broke away from his and he slid Apollyon and Serenity a look he hoped conveyed every ounce of his desire for them to be gone. The last thing he needed was an audience, and he didn't want either of them hearing him making love to Isadora.

This was a private moment, one he needed to be just about them.

Apollyon scowled at him.

The witch gently placed her hand on his arm and they both disappeared.

Rook lowered his head, kissed the curve of Isadora's throat and carried her into the bedroom.

He pressed one knee into the mattress and laid her down on it, covered her with his body and groaned as she rocked against him, the friction firmer now, enough to have shivers tripping through him whenever she rubbed the length of his cock through his jeans.

He needed them gone.

He needed her naked beneath him.

He focused and sent his clothes away, leaving him nude.

Isadora moaned and skimmed her fingers over his shoulders, her blue eyes darkening with need he could feel in her as she studied his body, tracing the lines of his muscles and leaving hot trails in the wake of her fingertips.

He caught her waist and shoved her up the covers, and kneeled on the bed, intending to settle himself over her again.

She sat up and pushed against his chest, forcing him to rise onto his knees before her.

Hell.

He stilled as she wrapped a hand around his shaft, as she pushed down to reveal the crown, and cupped his balls.

"Damn I missed you," she murmured, her voice tight, drenched with desire.

Talking to him, or his cock?

Her eyes lifted to meet his and he groaned as she fisted his length again, holding it tightly, squeezing it in a way that sent heat rolling through him, a hit of pleasure that robbed him of his breath.

He lowered his hands in response, cupped her breasts through her black dress and pinched her beaded nipples. Hard. She gasped, but pleasure lit her eyes, darkened them in a way that was too damn sexy.

He knew her.

Whether he remembered her or not.

He knew everything about her, all the things she loved, and yet he didn't know her.

And that was a weird feeling.

As he tweaked her nipples and she lowered her hand again to rub the spot beneath his sac, sending an intense wave of bliss through him that had his cock jerking in a way that brought a smile to her kiss-reddened lips, it struck him that she definitely knew him.

Hell, did she know him.

He lost focus as she went to war on him, brought her mouth to his cock and licked the length of it before taking him into her wet heat. He groaned as pleasure overwhelmed him, the feel of her mouth moving on him as she teased the spot behind his balls and played with them too much to handle. It quickly built, a tightness forming inside him, and he breathed harder as he struggled to survive the onslaught, to hold back his climax so she didn't know the power she had over him.

The wicked glint in her eyes as she quickly released him from the heaven of her mouth and firmly gripped his length, squeezing it hard just as he had been about to lose his battle, said there was no point in trying to pretend she didn't rule him.

She already knew she did.

Rook clutched her shoulders when she looked as if she might go to war on him again, unsure he could handle another round, not without finding release. Whatever she had done with her hand had stopped him, but he was perilously close to the edge, in danger of catapulting right over it the second she licked or stroked him again.

"A moment." He extricated himself from her grip and collapsed onto the bed beside her.

Isadora didn't give him what he wanted.

But damn, she gave him what he needed.

She rose onto her knees, stripped off her dress to reveal her lush bare curves, and crawled towards him.

He groaned, his eyebrows furrowing as she prowled towards him, looking as if she wanted to devour him.

His thighs trembled as she skimmed her hands up them and he reached above him, gripped the pillow and held it tightly behind his head as he watched her. Her silver hair tickled his thighs as she lowered her head and pressed slow kisses to his skin, and he bit back another groan as her breasts brushed his legs.

He wasn't sure whether to tip his head back and moan, or keep his eyes locked on her as she worked magic on him, teasing him and keeping him right at the edge with every soft kiss or hard nip. He wasn't sure whether he was coming or going as she swirled her tongue over his hip, brushed her palms up his thighs, and came close to touching his aching cock.

It kicked in response to the near miss of her fingers, and jerked again when she kissed near to it and her hair brushed it.

She was doing it on purpose.

His fault for saying he needed a moment?

She wasn't really giving him one. Now she had him on fire with a need for her to touch him, to stroke and lick him again. He was wild with another need too, a hunger to touch her, to tease her in return and wring sweet moans from her, knowing he was responsible for her pleasure.

He tried to reach her shoulder to pull her up to him so he could kiss her, could palm her breasts and torment her, but she evaded him, her smile growing mischievous.

Rook groaned as she dropped her head and licked the length of his shaft, from root to tip, her silver hair concealing her face and everything she was doing from view as it spilled over his stomach. Another groan tore from him as he looked at the peachy globes of her bottom where it jutted into the air, swaying side to side as she drove him out of his ever-loving mind.

He growled as she nipped at his cock, sending a hot wave of shivers rolling down it, and reached down to her, fisted her hair and pulled her head up. Her hunger-darkened gaze locked on his, unrepentant. She strained against his hold, her eyes remaining on his, and his breaths came faster as he watched her mouth nearing the head of his length. Her tongue darted out and he groaned as she teased him, softly stroked the crown and sent another shiver bolting through him.

Shit, he wasn't sure he could take much more.

She gasped as he hauled her up to him by her hair and claimed her mouth, swallowing the moan that followed it. Her body pressed against his, breasts scalding his chest, and he clamped his free hand down on her backside and held her to him as he rubbed his aching length against her damp curls.

"Need you," he uttered against her lips between rough kisses, echoing her earlier words.

Her legs fell down on either side of his hips and she sat back as he released her hair. Her eyes locked with his again as he skimmed his hands over the curve of her waist, and his breaths came faster as she rose off him, took hold of his length and eased it into position.

His ability to breathe shut off completely as she pressed back on his cock and the crown breached her hot core. His focus dropped to where they joined and he stared as she sank onto him, taking every inch of him into her, her breathing quickening as he filled her.

Hell.

He swallowed hard.

His cock kicked in her warm sheath, so tight with need he wasn't sure he would last more than a few strokes.

He groaned in time with her as she leaned over him, her body sliding up his length, and caught hold of his shoulders. He obeyed as she pulled him up into a sitting position and cupped her backside as his chest met hers again. She kissed him, softer now, and he focused on it, on the way her tight body gloved him and how sweet she tasted on his lips.

She brushed her palms over his cheeks, the gentleness of her caress sending heat of a different nature spiralling through him, warmth that filled his heart.

"Isadora," he murmured against her lips, lost in the way she was kissing him, how it stirred feelings he wasn't sure how to process because they were unfamiliar.

He had told her that he loved her, but the emotions that washed through him as he held her, their bodies entwined, ran so deep he wasn't sure he could label it as love. It transcended that emotion. She was vital to him, part of him that he had been missing for millennia, but now she was back.

She broke away from his lips, smiled softly, and suddenly gripped his hair and yanked his head back.

"Sweet fuck," he groaned and shuddered, and damn, what he felt for his little witch was definitely deeper than love.

She knew all the right buttons to press in him.

He growled, his teeth all sharpening in response to the pleasure that crashed over him as she fisted his hair, held it so tight his scalp stung, and began working her body on him, riding his cock with swirls of her hips that left him at her mercy.

Her breasts bounced against his chest as she rocked on him and he ripped a moan from her as he cupped them, as he rolled her nipples between his fingers and squeezed.

He lowered his left hand to her hip, clutched it and drove her down onto his cock as he tensed and thrust up into her. She moaned, pulled his head back and kissed him.

He tried to focus to shift his teeth back, fumbling the kiss as panic flashed through him.

"Don't," she muttered, her breath washing over his face. "I can handle them."

He shuddered and groaned as she stroked her tongue over his fangs, teasing him with the light caress. He growled and lifted his head, claimed her lips and tangled his tongue with hers as he brought her down onto him, harder than before.

She rewarded him with another moan, this one breathless, and followed it with a little cry as he drove into her. He twisted her nipple again, tearing another from her, and she gripped his shoulder with her other hand and moved faster, longer strokes that had his balls tightening again, release rising up his aching length.

Hell, he needed more.

He pumped his hips, faster now, desperately reaching for release as her cries filled his ears, bursting from her lips between kisses.

She tensed in his arms, her body clamping down on him, and threw her head back, her hoarse cry echoing around the room as her hips kicked forwards. He groaned as she quivered around him, her heart thundering in his ears, her sheath milking him as her heat scalded him.

Her hands slipped from his hair and his shoulder, and he caught her as she fell backwards. She was a picture as she lay on his legs, her arms splayed at her sides, breasts heaving as she fought for air. Quiet moans escaped her and her tongue swept out to chase over her reddened lips, making him want to pull her back up to him and kiss her again.

Only he couldn't move, was too fascinated by the feel of her body flexing around his, how it gripped him like a glove in her current position.

A lazy smile curled her lips as her eyes fluttered closed.

He grinned and skimmed one hand over her belly, pushed his thumb between her plush petals and teased her pert nub. She moaned, her face twisting with it as he rubbed her, teasing her as he kept his cock in her. Her teeth sank into her lower lip, her nipples beading again as he pushed her through the haze of her first climax.

He dropped his gaze to where he joined with her, a groan of his own rolling up his throat at the sight of him buried inside her. He glistened with her moisture. He lowered his thumb, caught some of it, and brought it back up, used it to tease her higher, stroking her bead until she was rocking against him, moving on his cock again.

This time, he wanted to be the one in control.

The moment she was writhing again, breathless little whimpers escaping her, he lifted her off his cock, twisted her onto her belly as she moaned her disapproval, and rose onto his knees as he set her down on the bed. He kicked her legs apart, pulled her hips up and fed his cock into her, sliding as deep as she could take him.

She pressed back against him, on her hands and knees, a contented sigh leaving her lips as he filled and stretched her again.

He skimmed his hand up her spine, buried his fingers into her silver hair, and twisted it in his fist.

A moan burst from her lips as he tugged on it, pulling her head back, and gripped her hip with his other hand. He tore another from her as he thrust into her, withdrew almost all the way and plunged back in again. He held her immobile as he drove into her, his pace building until he couldn't go any faster, was furiously pumping her, filling her over and over as she began to tighten around him.

Her moans filled the room, mingling with his own grunts as he pulled on her hair and gripped her hip, his fingers digging into her soft flesh.

"More," she barked and pressed back against him.

He groaned and plunged deeper, faster, giving her all of him, everything he could as release rose to the base of his cock.

The sight of her at his mercy, the pleasure he could feel building in her, one that told him she enjoyed being under his command as much as he had loved being under hers, was too much.

He grunted and shoved as deep as he could go as his entire body quaked with the force of his release and his cock kicked, throbbed in time with each jet of his seed into her. His legs shook, the bliss rolling through him so intense that his breath seized in his throat and stars winked across his vision as he held Isadora on him.

She moaned, her body milking his, thighs quivering as violently as his own were as she remained locked against him.

"Damn," she breathed and sank onto her front on the bed when he found the ability to work muscle and bone again and released her hair. "I really did miss that."

Rook felt sure that if he had remembered it, he would have missed it too.

His only experience of love was witnessing the mushy kind that Apollyon obviously shared with Serenity.

He hadn't expected love could be this consuming, this powerful and commanding.

He stroked his hand down Isadora's spine, his gaze lingering on her as she tilted her head to her right and a smile stretched her lips, a soft sigh escaping them as she slowly came down with him.

He hadn't expected making love could drive him so wild or leave him this shaken.

He wasn't sure he would ever be the same again.

He grinned, leaned over her and peppered her back with kisses.

He was sure of something though.

The night was young.

And they were only just getting started.

# CHAPTER 16

Isadora smiled as she woke, stretched up and hugged the pillow. She swivelled her head and bit her lip as she buried her face in it, a moan rolling up her throat as a skilled tongue teased her between her thighs.

Best wake up call ever.

She grinned and tried to keep still as Rook swept his tongue over her arousal, flicked it and laved it, sending sparks skittering over her thighs and up her belly.

"Morning," he husked, voice gravelly and low, and before she could answer, he licked her again, tearing a moan from her.

The angel was insatiable.

She had lost count of the number of times they had made love last night, was fairly certain they had covered almost every position possible, and might have invented some new ones.

Her grin widened.

Rook always had been inventive, and passionate, doing everything at full throttle.

Apart from now, as he languidly explored her with his tongue, slowly teasing her towards a climax.

She stretched out, savouring the calm of it and how it gently built inside her, unhurried and incredibly sensual, awakening every inch of her in a way she wasn't sure she had experienced before.

She loved the wild side of Rook, the one that matched hers, but she could easily come to love this softer side of him just as much.

She moaned into the pillow, because as much as Rook was stealing her focus with his worship of her body, she could sense that Serenity and Apollyon had returned, and she *really* didn't want them sharing her wake up call.

It had been embarrassing enough when they had seen Rook carrying her to the bedroom last night.

She bit the pillow, muffling another moan as Rook skimmed a finger down her inner thigh and anticipation swirled inside her, an ache for him to ease it into her and bring her to climax.

He stroked it over where she needed him, teasing her.

When he did it again, she grabbed another pillow and hit him with it. He chuckled, the warm sound chasing away her anger, and brought his fingers back towards her core.

He stiffened at the same time as she tensed.

Something was coming.

Something powerful.

Rook popped to his knees, deliciously and distractingly naked as the covers fell away from him.

It wasn't anything born of his realm.

This danger was born of hers.

"Dress," he growled, his eyes gaining a crimson glow as the skin around them darkened.

Armour materialised on his body, the scarlet-edged obsidian plates moulding over his chest first, followed by the pointed slats that protected his hips over his loincloth. His vambraces appeared on his forearms as he rolled from the bed, and just as his bare feet hit the wooden floor, black leather boots formed on them and his greaves materialised over his shins.

Isadora scurried off the bed and grabbed her dress. She pulled it on, wrestling with it as panic started as a low drumming in her veins but quickly escalated into a full-on pounding that had her pulse racing.

She knew that power.

Bitch and Spanish Inquisition were close.

A crimson blade formed in Rook's hand and he held his free one out to her as scarlet wings erupted from his back.

She muttered a spell to make her boots appear on her feet and another to produce a silver chest piece that moulded to her breasts over her black dress.

Rook glanced at her and lingered, his eyes fixed on her chest. They darkened, hunger igniting in them.

"Later." She tugged on his hand, pulling him towards the door, because it really wasn't the time for him to get hot and bothered by the sight of her in form-fitting armour.

He took the lead, guiding her out into the main room of the apartment where Apollyon stood dressed in his gold-edged onyx armour, his black wings furled against his back and twin gold blades gripped tightly on either side of his hips.

Serenity stood close to him near the open door to the kitchen, her pretty cream dress making her look out of place against the grim backdrop of her angel of death.

The petite blonde muttered words beneath her breath as red magic swirled around her hands, sparking in places as the ribbons twisted and collided.

Isadora broke free of Rook's grip and went to her. She took hold of Serenity's hand and chanted with her, linking their power to make the spell stronger.

Hopefully as strong as they needed it to be.

"What should I be expecting here?" Rook came up beside her, his blade at the ready and his crimson eyes locked on the French doors that led onto the terrace.

She focused on the world outside, on the disturbance she had felt, power that unnerved her, setting her on edge and filling her mind with doubts. She shut them down, refusing to let them shake her. She was strong now, her magic free of the shackles that had bound it, and she wasn't alone. Rook was with her, and so was Apollyon and Serenity. She had another powerful witch at her side, and two extremely powerful angels.

They could handle what was coming.

"There were two more witches in the group. A male, powerful and competent, and a female," she quickly said and then returned to chanting the spell with Serenity. She focused on the spell, keeping her magic flowing into it as she glanced at Rook. "The female... she's Country Estate's sister. The leader."

Serenity lifted her free hand and Isadora followed suit as the spell built around her hand, formed and strained for release. Not yet, they needed it stronger.

"Not good. I'm figuring she's more powerful than the others?" Rook placed his hand on her shoulder when she nodded and she silently thanked him for the boost as her magic hungrily reached for the connection between them and siphoned some of his power.

She silently thanked him for being concerned about her too.

He wanted her stronger, wanted her to have as much power as she could handle so she would be safe. She could feel it as her magic connected to him, revealing his feelings to her.

"How did they find you?" Apollyon moved closer to Serenity and Isadora felt it when he connected with her, providing a boost to her magic too.

"Shit," Isadora growled as it hit her. "My magic."

It was possible one of the spells that had been cast on her by the group had been a sort of tracker, one that triggered whenever she used her power. She had probably sounded the alarm when she had fought Country Estate, and again yesterday when she had revealed her markings.

Her eyes widened and she lowered them to her hand and the spell whizzing around it.

She was giving them her exact bloody location.

"We have to stop." She whipped around to face Serenity. "I think they have a tracer on my magic."

The sensation of dark power that rang in the air suddenly grew stronger.

"Too late," Serenity whispered.

Isadora hurled the spell with her, desperate to provide them with some protection, a shield that would hopefully keep the witches at bay.

The crimson globe exploded in size, sweeping outwards from their hands to engulf the apartment and disappear into the floor and ceiling, forming a barrier around them.

Serenity tossed her a worried look and Isadora knew why. No magic could pass through the barrier in either direction, and that included teleporting. It would bounce them back into the bubble. They were trapped, but they were safe, and right now that was all she cared about.

"Help me get rid of this spell." She turned to Serenity and the blonde took hold of her hands.

Isadora closed her eyes and worked with Serenity, seeking the spell that had given the witches her location, aware they were growing closer by the second. She could feel them through the barrier, their dark magic spreading in the air around them, slowly gaining strength as they searched the vicinity for her.

"Got it." Serenity tightened her grip on Isadora's hands and began chanting.

Light pulsed through Isadora in golden waves that grew brighter and stronger as she listened to Serenity's words, let them soak into her and draw out the spell. It writhed inside her, dark and malevolent, a vicious thorny thing that tugged at her and tried to sink back into her bones whenever Serenity's strength slipped.

Isadora began to chant with her, put force into each word that drained her strength but struck at the spell too, weakening it. She gritted her teeth and cried out through them as it ripped from her, pushed out by the counter spell.

She sagged and strong arms caught her, keeping her upright.

"You good?" Rook murmured close to her ear as she settled with her back against his chest and she nodded. "Then we're getting out of here."

"How—" She cut herself off as she looked up at him, her words about how teleportation magic wouldn't work because of the barrier dying on her lips.

A shimmering white portal blazed behind him.

She stared at it and then at him.

"Perk of the job?" He offered, an awkward edge to his expression. "Sometimes it pays to be a bad angel."

She wasn't going to argue with that, not when an incredible force hit the barrier, shook the building and sent her staggering forwards.

"This is not good," Serenity said and Isadora didn't need to look to see what had her worried now, could feel it as spells pounded against the red shield.

The barrier wasn't going to hold out for long against that level of offensive magic. Spanish Inquisition and Bitch were far more powerful than she had believed. Doubt slithered through her again, forming ice along the line of her spine.

"Leaving now." Rook wrapped his arm around her stomach and hauled her backwards into the portal.

Apollyon pulled Serenity in behind them.

Isadora's eyes widened as a violet glow lit the room. "Faster!"

The scent of snow swirled around her and she felt the forest and the ancient mountains. Rook swept her around to clear the portal and Apollyon leaped through it with Serenity, landing on the pristine white of the lake beside them.

The portal shrank, quickly closing as Rook held his left hand out towards it.

But not quickly enough.

She braced against him as a violet orb shot through the tiny remnant of the portal and detonated, showering the area in lilac sparks that shone in the early morning light.

"Another tracker." She glared at the glittering pieces of it as they drifted around her, catching the gentle breeze and slowly dancing towards the snowy ground.

They settled on her too, and on Apollyon and Serenity.

Rook huffed and brushed them off him, his lip curling to flash sharp teeth. "Can you cancel it out or something?"

"No."

He frowned at her. "No? You reversed the other spell."

"This one is different. It caused a blanket effect when it detonated, transforming one spell into... like... a million tiny spells." She did her best to sweep the purple flakes off her clothes, but just like non-magical glitter, it got everywhere and refused to go away. "I'm going to be finding bits of this spell for days... which is about as long as this spell will last. They'll keep finding us until it wears off."

Rook's face darkened, black emerging around his crimson eyes, and his deep voice had a cold edge to it as he scowled at the point where the portal had been. "Or until I kill them."

His forearms blackened and she took a step back as he grew in size, muscles bulging beneath his darkening skin.

His focus whipped to his right and his crimson eyes narrowed.

Her gaze leaped there.

There was only the lake and the forest, with the mountains rising beyond it to pierce the blue sky, the snow that capped them shining in the sunlight.

Two figures appeared right where Rook had been looking.

Damn, his senses were sharp, far sharper than they had been when he had been a guardian angel.

He grunted and shifted to face the brunette female and the ice-blond male who stood beside her.

Bitch swept her wavy hair over her shoulder, revealing a low-cut crimson top that was more suited to a nightclub than the frozen wilderness. She scowled at Isadora, her dark brown eyes holding every drop of the anger Isadora could feel in her.

She probably deserved it for killing her brother, but she wasn't going to regret what she had done, or what she was about to do.

The woman strode forwards, long black-leather-clad legs carrying her with confidence towards them.

Her dark gaze slid to Rook, Apollyon and Serenity, and then back to Isadora. "So... which one do I need to kill to make you give me that spell?"

Rook snarled, flashing his fangs as his transformation completed, the feathers of his wings falling away to reveal the leathery membrane beneath.

Bitch smiled at him.

Isadora snapped.

Darkness poured through her, a rage so deep and powerful she couldn't contain it. The pain of losing him all those centuries ago combined with the terror she had felt when he had gone through the ice and had almost slipped from her grasp once more. Magic surged in response, lit up her blood and stole her breath as she wrestled for control, fighting a battle she knew she wouldn't win.

Because she couldn't lose Rook.

Which meant this bitch had to die.

# CHAPTER 17

Isadora launched her hand forwards, a silver ball of magic bursting from it with barely a thought from her as the need to protect Rook seized hold of her. She followed it with another and then another, hurling them at the witch. The brunette dodged them all with ease, deflecting them with spells of her own and sending them flying in all directions.

Rook swept his hand down his blade and it grew in size, becoming a sword more worthy of his demonic stature. He growled and lumbered forwards, his heavy footfalls shaking the ice as he set his sights on the woman.

Still as reckless as ever.

"Go," Apollyon barked and she nodded, didn't hesitate to chase after him as the witch noticed Rook and smiled, as if her victory had just been assured and the spell was already within her grasp.

Spanish Inquisition hurled three smaller spells at Rook. They hovered above his hand for a heartbeat, illuminating the harsh planes of his face and casting white light over his dark violet dress shirt, and then shot towards Rook. They twirled and zoomed around each other, forming a spiral of light as they closed in on her angel.

Isadora focused on them, conjuring a counter-attack.

Twin blue orbs shot past her and collided with them, knocking them off course, sending them whizzing towards Bitch.

"We can handle him," Serenity called and Isadora shifted her focus to the woman.

The brunette raised her hands before her and a black-purple barrier formed in front of them just as the rogue spells reached her. She grunted as they slammed against it, the force of the blow sending her staggering backwards and skidding across the ice of the lake.

Rook ploughed into her before she could recover, his shoulder slamming into her gut and lifting her off the ice. He growled and thrust with his blade, but she swept her hand down, moving the barrier spell with it, and blocked him.

His sword connected with the spell.

Isadora's eyes widened as he went flying in a tangle of limbs and wings that made it impossible to tell which end of him was which as he spun. He shook his head and snarled as he finally managed to unfurl his wings and beat them, heading back towards Bitch.

Black vines shot up from the ground, snaking towards him.

Rook growled as he hacked at them, trying to stop them from reaching him, and snarled as one latched around his leg and yanked him down, slamming him into the ice.

Isadora growled with him, her gaze snapping to the witch.

Bitch would pay for that.

She lifted her hands and shards of ice burst from the snow, racing in a line towards the witch. A grin curved her lips when the witch kept her focus on Rook as she waved her hands around before her, commanding the vine that held Rook, lifting him back into the air with it.

The spikes of ice closed in on her.

Rook suddenly crashed into them like a wrecking ball, shattering them and sending them shooting across the lake.

Towards Apollyon and Serenity where they were locked in a battle with Spanish Inquisition.

"Look out!" she called and the blonde twirled to face her, her hazel eyes going round as she spotted the long javelins of ice rocketing through the air towards her.

She held both hands out in front of her and a barrier flickered in front of them. Isadora's heart lodged in her throat. It wasn't going to solidify fast enough.

She called on her own magic and hurled her hands forwards, preparing to unleash a wave of fire in Serenity's direction and praying it would reach her in time.

The spell died on her lips as a dazzling beam of golden light swept across the lake between Serenity and the shards of ice, the heat of it so fierce that the water steamed as it gushed upwards and over the frozen lake.

Serenity staggered backwards, breathing hard as her head whipped up, her eyes locking on the sky.

Isadora looked there.

Apollyon hovered above her, his blades crossed before him and golden light crackling around them. The beam stuttered and faded, leaving a long gash in the lake.

The blond witch looked as if he was having second thoughts as he stared at Apollyon, his face pale and grey eyes enormous.

Serenity didn't give him a chance to run. She thrust her hand towards him, sending three spears of blue at him. He hurled himself to his right, narrowly evading them, and they ploughed into the snowy forest, sending a plume of white up into the air.

Apollyon swept down, landing beside Serenity, and furled his wings as he advanced on the male.

Rook grunted, snagging Isadora's attention. He hacked at the vine and Isadora ran over to him, reaching him just as Bitch tried to use the black roots to take hold of him again. Isadora planted her hands against them and let the spell that had been building inside her loose on them instead. Green light zoomed along their lengths, and they rapidly withered, turning to ashes before her eyes.

The witch screamed as the fire reached the roots, the point where it connected her to the spell, and green light swept over her. She lifted her hands before her and stared at them as her skin lost some of its colour, the spell affecting her as it had the vines, sapping the life from her.

"Enrique," she muttered as she sank to her knees, her dark eyes enormous, flooded with fear.

The male pivoted to look at her, his face a black mask. "Damn you."

Isadora wasn't sure whether that was aimed at her for hurting the witch, or at the witch for using his name, giving it to her.

Serenity leaped on it before she could, wove it into a spell and tied it to him before she launched it in his direction. He tried to evade it, ran and dodged, fired spells of his own, but it chased him, zigzagging whenever he did.

Isadora wanted to grin when it finally slammed into him, exploding in a bright flash, but her smile faltered as the air cleared, revealing the male where he lay prone on the ice, his black jeans and dark shirt flecked with snow.

Down but not dead.

"Sorry... I..." Serenity muttered in French, her voice dripping with apology.

Isadora helped Rook onto his feet and shot her a look she hoped conveyed that she wasn't going to hold it against her. Not everyone was cut out for killing. She had been like that once, so long ago that she barely remembered those days.

She wasn't as forgiving now, had been forged into something harder by her years and experiences. She knew better than to leave an enemy alive.

She didn't have to worry about the male though.

Before she could raise a finger or utter a single syllable of a spell, Apollyon had landed hard beside the male and driven one of his blades right through him.

Bitch shrieked at him and launched to her feet, and swept her hands out in front of her, bringing them together before her. Black stilted ribbons burst from them in a swift beam heading straight for Apollyon's back.

"Mon ange!" Serenity screamed, her fear washing over Isadora together with her magic as it rose in response to the sight of her angel in danger.

Apollyon looked at her and disappeared, reappearing beside her, out of the path of the spell. Serenity cursed him and threw herself into his arms, and he wrapped her in his wings as he held her.

"I am harder to kill than that," he murmured and brushed his lips across her golden hair.

Isadora's eyes widened as Bitch grunted and slowly turned on her heel, shifting the path of the beam. It snapped at the ice as it cut through the air, closing in on Apollyon and Serenity.

"I'm getting bored of all this long range hocus pocus," Rook growled, dipped down towards the ice, and kicked off, causing the sheet they were on to rock violently as he launched into the air.

She struggled for balance, staggering towards the melted strip of lake that separated her from Apollyon and Serenity. "Move it you two."

Apollyon swept Serenity up into his arms and shot into the air with her, carrying her above the path of the beam.

Leaving it coming directly at Isadora.

"Shit."

She turned, skidded on the wet ice and slammed face-first into it, knocking the air from her lungs.

Her heart hammered against her chest as she looked over her shoulder.

The beam reached the edge of the ice on her side of the lake.

She tried to teleport, but the spell failed as fear combined with the drain of battling with her magic. She kicked off instead, cursing when she couldn't get any traction on the ice. The wave of power surrounding the spell reached her and she made the mistake of looking back at it as she finally found her feet.

She wasn't going to be fast enough.

She muttered a barrier, the strongest one she knew that could be conjured quickly, twisted and held her hands out in front of her, bracing herself for a direct hit.

The black beam fizzled and died.

Isadora stared at where it had been, shock rippling through her as she struggled to make sense of what had just happened and her fear flooding from her, leaving her legs weak beneath her.

She shifted her gaze to her right.

Rook looked at something in his left hand, shrugged and casually tossed it over his shoulder.

It skidded across the ice to stop a few metres from her and she baulked when she realised what it was.

A hand.

Rook's solution to stopping the witch from being able to use magic was sound in a way.

His own little way.

He saw magic as something that came from hands, and so he was going to remove them from the witch to stop her from using spells on him and the others, giving himself an opening to land a killing blow with his sword.

She cringed as he sailed through the air to land a few feet from her, copper sparks leaping from the front of his breastplate as he slid through the snow. It bunched around his shoulders, burying his dragon-like wings, and he almost disappeared beneath a bank of it as he finally stopped near her.

He grunted, growled and flashed fangs as he scowled and clawed his way out of the mound of snow.

"You know magic comes from inside us, right?" She hurried to him and offered her hand to him. He just glared at it and continued to fight his way out alone. She sighed. "Hands are just a way of directing the magic."

She proved it by hurling a spell at the bitch without looking at her or moving a muscle, sending the gold and blue orbs rocketing towards her at a speed she couldn't dodge. They struck her hard, knocking her flying, and she shrieked as she hit the ice, the vibrations from her impact reaching Isadora where she stood over Rook.

He huffed, lumbered onto his feet to tower at least three feet taller than her and snarled at her, exposing all red teeth as his crimson eyes narrowed on her.

"Fair enough." She wasn't going to argue with him, not when it was clear he wasn't in the mood for a lecture. "You do your thing, I'll do mine… like a team."

He paused, his expression twisting in a way that looked like a grimace but she presumed was his thinking face when he was demonic.

He nodded and held his hand out to her.

Expecting her to shake on it?

She shrugged and placed her hand in his big black one, shrieked like a damned girl when he hauled her into the air, twisted her and planted her bottom on his wide shoulder. She gripped his black hair in her right hand and wobbled, struggling to find her balance as he stomped towards the witch.

When she had talked about working together, she hadn't meant in such close proximity. She preferred a little distance when she was fighting, room to manoeuvre.

She certainly hadn't imagined she would be riding into battle on his shoulder.

He grunted and flexed his fingers around his broadsword, and she almost slid off his shoulder. She grabbed his chest plate to stop herself from falling and leaned into him, smothering the side of his head with her own breastplate.

He slid her a look as she righted herself, regaining her balance.

"Later," he grumbled, voice deeper than before but somehow still managing to hold a teasing note.

She cuffed him around the back of his head. "I'll give you later."

"You'll give it to me later?" He grinned at her and avoided her second blow.

Bright blue light burst out of the corner of her eye and she looked there.

A dome formed over the witch as she clutched the arm that was missing a hand to her. Blood spilled down it, matching the colour of her top. It dripped from her elbow and soaked into the snow and ice. Her lips drew back in a grimace, the power that flowed from her darkening as she glanced off to her right, towards the dead man.

Isadora refused to feel guilt over what had happened, just as she refused to feel guilt over what she was going to do next. It was this witch or her, and while she knew it wouldn't stop others from coming after her, she was going to put an end to this right here and right now.

And she wasn't going to feel an ounce of regret about it.

Rook rapped his knuckles against the dome, causing a hollow 'thunk' to echo around it, and looked up at her. "Portal?"

"No need." She leaned forwards, stretching towards the barrier, and pressed her palm against it as she took hold of Rook's nape with her other hand. Not to keep her steady, but to steal a little of his power.

It was stronger than expected, lit her up like a thunderbolt as her magic connected with him. Fire flowed into her, a raging torrent that had her feeling as if she might burst if she didn't find an outlet for all the power zinging through her.

She focused it on the barrier and ran through all the reversal spells she knew. They were quick to come, eager to devour the power she was feeding them. She barely had time to think about them before they were bursting from her, hitting the barrier like a barrage.

It crumbled before her and she wasn't sure which spell had been the right one, was left dazed and stunned by what just a small hit of Rook's power could do for her when he was fully demonic.

She had always been of the light, but damn, the dark was powerful and she could see why some witches went down that route.

The feel of Rook's strength flowing through her was addictive.

Incredible.

A little arousing.

He grinned up at her, as if he knew her thoughts. Or maybe he had felt it in her.

She pushed off from his shoulder to land squarely on her feet and focused as Bitch conjured more spells, smaller barriers that Isadora easily defeated, keeping her open as she advanced on her with Rook at her side.

The woman tossed another glance at the dead male and suddenly broke right as she hurled five golden orbs at her and Rook. Isadora sent two spells flying, one that formed a shield that curved before her, and another that chased after the witch.

That spell she hadn't needed.

Flakes of snow swirled in the air around her as Rook beat his wings and shot after the witch, skimming low above the ice. He was breathtaking as he banked right, revealing the full breadth of his black dragon-like wings, swept around behind the witch, coming out of the move on the other side of her, and rose before her in one fluid motion.

His hands moved so fast she couldn't track them, a crimson blur slicing through the air between him and the witch.

For a moment, Isadora was convinced he had missed.

The spells Bitch had cast at her detonated on the barrier protecting her, sending a shockwave blasting outwards across the ice. They struck the witch and buffeted Rook, but he remained standing, his sword still held out at his side.

Bitch toppled.

Rook casually flicked his wrist, sending blood splattering across the snow from his blade.

Isadora pulled a face as the brunette's head rolled away from her body, landing face up, her dark eyes locked sightlessly on the sky.

Some things were definitely different about her angel.

"You were always more of a stick them in the chest kind of man." She lowered the barrier, letting the magic fade.

The darkness washed from his skin, leaving it golden, and he shrank back to his normal size. Feathers sprouted on his wings, black at first, but slowly turning crimson as they grew.

He swept his hand over his blade, transforming it back into a short sword, and sheathed it as he shrugged. "Call it years of rising through the ranks in battles. You learn to be more efficient and make sure your enemy dies fast so you get noticed."

Isadora moved past him and he turned, the feel of his eyes on her as he tracked her heating her.

"What are you doing?" he said as Apollyon landed with Serenity.

She swallowed the bile that rose up her throat and crouched near the witch's severed head. "Serenity... can you help me?"

Serenity moved towards her but hesitated a short distance away, her eyes on the head. "It's risky to steal her magic."

And it was one she was willing to take.

She looked up at the blonde. "I don't know much in the way of dark magic, and there's a chance that some of her knowledge could help me with Rook's curse."

"No... I don't want you to do it." Rook swiftly closed the distance between them and took hold of her shoulder, his grip firm. "I don't need my memories, Isadora. We can make new ones."

She knew that, but she still needed to do this. "I want to get them back for you. I know it bothers you, Rook. It bothered me when I couldn't remember you."

He huffed and it became a sigh as she looked over her shoulder at him, right into his eyes, daring him to deny it. "Fine... it bothers me a little... but not as much as the thought of you risking yourself for my sake."

She placed her hand over his and gently squeezed it. "I'll only take a little knowledge... the spells that come easily... but it will mean it might take me longer to free your memories because I held back and didn't take it all."

He kneeled beside her, bringing his eyes level with hers, and twisted his hand beneath hers, so he was holding it as he gave her a slight smile. "We have all the time in the world... I'm not going anywhere. I'm right where I want to be."

She would have smiled at him for that, but Apollyon made a low noise in his throat that sounded distinctly like faux retching.

She glared at him at the same time as Rook growled and bared his fangs.

"Ignore him." Serenity took hold of her hand and placed it on the head, her face twisting in disgust as they both made contact.

Isadora closed her eyes and focused, let her magic pour into the witch's dying mind and burrow deep. She plucked the spells from it, the ones that were lured to her magic, desperate to escape into a living host, and snatched a few others, ones that put up a fight and she wasn't going to tell Rook about.

Ones that could prove dangerous to her.

She wouldn't attempt to use them until she had a grasp of dark magic and was able to control them, and then she would find a way to tame them so they wouldn't turn on her.

She broke contact with the witch and sat back, loosing her breath in a long sigh as fatigue swept through her and she struggled with the new spells, trying to get them to settle within her mind. One or two wanted to be used immediately on their former host. She quietened those but it took effort that left her drained, and she didn't resist Rook as he helped her onto her feet and held her close to him, banding one thick arm around her waist to support her.

"What will you do now?" Apollyon looked between her and Rook. "The Devil can't command you… Isadora is clearly your master… but he *can* find you."

And that meant he could try to get the location of the talisman and the one it protected from her again.

"We'll run," Rook said.

Surprise washed through her and her eyes leaped to his face.

He frowned down at her. "What?"

"We talked about running away once." Had he remembered that?

His gaze grew heated, and she could see in it that even if he didn't have the memory of that moment, a part of him that was buried deep recalled it.

It had been after they had made love and had been holding each other, utterly spent, and she had traced patterns on his chest and had asked him whether he would ever leave his duty behind for her.

He had told her that he would. He would run to the ends of the Earth with her. For her. He would do anything to be with her.

After that, she had bound them with the spell, a sign of their eternal love.

They had planned to run that night, but she had foolishly gone to meet with the people, wanting a clear conscience when she disappeared with Rook. She had needed to know the one she had crafted the talisman for would be safe, and had ended up falling into the Devil's hands.

She looked up at Rook, deep into his turquoise eyes. "Will you run with me now? We could have that quiet forever after together."

He framed her face, gently holding her cheeks in his warm palms, and nodded as he gazed down at her. "I would do anything for you, Isadora."

She tiptoed and kissed him, savoured the warmth of his lips against hers and how he wrapped his arms around her, pinning her to him.

It was hard to convince herself to let him go, but she managed it. She broke the kiss, pressed against his chest and stepped back from him. He released her but kept one arm around her waist, keeping her close to him.

She focused on her hands, on a spell, and cupped them, one above the other. When she opened her hands, a small silver pendant of angel's wings sat on her palm.

"If you ever need us... use it to call on us." She offered the talisman to Serenity.

Serenity took it, nodded and smiled. "I will listen to the grapevine in Paris... will do my best to turn the rumours about you and the binding spell into just that... a rumour. One I hope will fade with time so you'll be free again."

She slipped out of Rook's grip and hugged her. "Be careful."

"If you ever need us, you know where to find me. You do not remember, but we are brothers of a sort, bound by our pasts... a time when we had been a team. All of us worked to protect Isadora back then, and all of us will work to protect her, and you, now. You are not alone. Myself, Einar and Lukas will always be there for you. It is good to have you back again." Apollyon clutched Rook's shoulder, and she hid her smile as Rook looked as if he either wanted to punch the angel or shed a manly tear.

She couldn't decide which it was as he nodded and stiffly patted Apollyon's shoulder.

He was quick to gather her into his arms as soon as the angel released him though, cradled her to him as he held his left hand out and darkness swirled in the air, gathering speed before it suddenly burst into white flames and formed a portal.

She barely had a chance to wave at Serenity and Apollyon as Rook swept her up into his arms and carried her into it. They appeared in a desert, and then he stepped into another portal, and then another, until she grew dizzy and focused on him instead of the places they passed through.

She wrapped her arms around his neck and held him, studied his profile as he focused on making it impossible for anyone to track them, protecting her in his own way, one that told her just how much he loved her and wanted to keep her safe.

She was safe, for now, and when they finally found a place to settle, she would use all of her power to make sure they were safe forever. She would shield them from witches and the Devil himself. She would protect them in her own way.

And she wouldn't let anything part them again.

Because that forever they had promised each other finally started now.

# CHAPTER 18

Spring had rolled in at some point. Crisp air swept in through the open door of the cabin and Isadora breathed deep of it, savoured the freshness and the cold bite it still held as she moved around the kitchen area. Behind her, the fire crackled and popped, the heat of it keeping the chill at bay as she poured hot water into her mug.

She set the kettle back on the stove and walked to the calendar Rook had hung on a nail near the door to the bathroom, picked up the pen that dangled from a string and put a line through yesterday.

She stared at the date.

Six months.

It had been six months since Rook had blasted back into her life and they had put an end to the group who had been after the spell that bound them, and every single day with him had been bliss, passed peacefully in their new home.

She wasn't a fool anymore. The peace they were enjoying wouldn't last forever, even when she hoped that it would. Eventually, someone would follow a lead on her or Rook, and they would work hard enough to get past every decoy and false rumour she and Rook had spread across the globe with the help of Serenity and Apollyon, and their friends.

One day, someone would find them.

And that was fine.

They were prepared.

That day wouldn't be the end of her and Rook's life together.

It would be the end of the intruder's life.

Isadora carried her violently pink and yellow spotted mug with her as she moved back through the kitchen towards the door, drawn there by her new favourite sound.

The methodical thud and oh-so-masculine grunt that accompanied it always drew her to the porch so she could admire him.

As her slippers hit the deck, she was greeted by the stunning sight of Rook working in the small clearing in the dense forest. The lake that glittered in the sunlight beyond their sloping yard and the snow-capped mountains that rose on the other side of it into the clear blue sky added a breathtaking finishing touch to the scene.

Would she ever stop feeling free whenever she stood in this spot, breathed in the clean air and felt the hum of magic in everything around her?

They had ventured deep into the Canadian wilderness to find this place, one that had instantly felt like home and where they could finally settle. It was miles from the nearest town, and far off the beaten track. She hadn't seen a soul other than Rook in the area in all the months they had been here.

It was just her and him.

And that made it perfect.

She hugged her mug of tea to her black woollen jumper as she watched that slice of perfection working, his muscles shifting deliciously beneath his golden skin as he brought the axe over his head in a fast arc and it sliced clean through the log he had placed on the chopping block.

Perfection.

"You could do this with a spell," he grumbled and she smiled at how annoyed he sounded.

It was all an act, one designed to draw the response he wanted to hear from her.

She shrugged and sipped her tea. "But then I wouldn't get to watch you."

He grinned at that, and damn, he was returning to the angel he had been all those years ago when they had first met. Less serious and far more mischievous and wicked. Devastatingly sexy.

He positioned another log, taking his time about it, letting her drink her fill of the sight of him, and then hefted his axe above his head and paused, his dark turquoise gaze sliding to her.

"You have me chopping wood so much I'm not surprised you're always so feisty." His grin stretched wider as he tightened his grip, causing every muscle to flex and sending a bolt of heat right through her, one that made her want to bite her lip and press her thighs together.

Damn him.

"It's a strange form of foreplay if you ask me." He casually lowered the axe, gripping it in both hands, one at the base of the handle and one near the blade.

Isadora shook her head and held back her smile. "I can go inside if you want."

"Stay right there," he growled and swung the axe, slamming it into the chopping block beside the log.

She wasn't sure she could have moved even if she had wanted to as he prowled towards her, his eyes darkening rapidly, filling with need that echoed her own. Mother Earth, she swore he was sexier now than he had been as a guardian angel, brash and confident in his own skin, aware that he was powerful and strong, and that she loved it.

Heat flashed through her as he stalked towards her, moving slowly, his eyes locked on her the entire time, filled with a look that said he wanted to devour her.

She certainly wanted to devour him.

He mounted the steps to the deck, grabbed her around her hips as he reached the last one and lifted her. She quickly held her tea out to her side, away from him as it spilled, and chastised him with a look.

He just grinned at her and the mug disappeared from her hand.

"That was my favourite mug." She cuffed him playfully around his head, earning a glare from him.

"It's hideous," he muttered and it reappeared on the small wooden table beside their chairs.

Rook had positioned their cabin perfectly so they could watch the sunset together from the deck and she loved lazing there with him, recovering from their sessions.

She lowered her hands and skimmed her fingers over the new ink on his forearms, two thin bands that ran around them just above the spell that bound them together. It was the first spell she had learned from the books they had been stealing from every coven around the globe, using his ability to cast portals to get them in and out without the witches sensing them.

The book that had contained this spell had been in one of the oldest covens in Italy, and she was sure they weren't happy about the fact it had disappeared without a trace, but she didn't care.

It kept Rook safe.

It kept him hidden from everyone but her, and it had been made possible by the first memory of his that she had unlocked when they had been building their home, one that had confirmed something Apollyon had said.

The Devil wasn't Rook's master.

She was.

It had taken Rook a few days to get over the release of the first few memories, so they had been doing it little by little, one session every week. The first memory she had unlocked for him had shaken him the worst, but he was quicker to process each new one they freed.

"You're thinking about it again." He lowered her to her feet and brushed his palms over her cheeks, framing her face and tipping her head up so she was looking into his eyes. He sighed, the soft sound conveying a wealth of emotion. "It wasn't your fault, Isadora."

But it was.

He could tell her that it wasn't all he wanted, but it wouldn't stop her from feeling guilty about what had happened to him.

Rook had fallen when he had thought she had died.

But unlike other angels, falling into service of the Devil hadn't been the catalyst for the change that had come over him.

He had been so distraught and enraged that he had fought the Devil, desperate for revenge, to claim the head of the one who had taken her from him. The torture he had endured had taken its toll on him though, and the Devil had easily defeated him, subduing him again and locking him in a lightless cell.

The pain of losing her had awoken a darkness in Rook, one so powerful that it had swiftly devoured all the light in him, turning him into a demonic angel.

"You fell because of me," she whispered and smoothed her palms over his thick onyx hair, her eyebrows furrowing as she thought about all the pain he had gone through, how terrible it must have been in order to cause the darkness to take hold of him and vanquish the light.

The Devil had been quick to use a witch to take his memories of what had happened, fooling Rook into believing he served him like all the other Hell's angels, when he had still been hers to command.

She blamed herself for the fact the Devil had taken his memories from him.

She had escaped and the Devil had needed to keep him in his possession, so he could use Rook as leverage when he found her again, sure that she would do whatever he wanted when she realised that Rook was alive.

Rook dipped his head and swept his lips across her cheek, and she frowned at him as he pulled back.

"I hate seeing you cry." He gave her a tight smile, his dark eyebrows furrowing as he gazed down at her. "We're together now. Stronger for everything that has happened... think of it that way."

She nodded and sniffled, scrubbed her hands across her cheeks and drew down a deep breath. She wasn't going to cry, not again. She had done some serious ugly crying when she had unlocked those memories for him. Rook had teased her for days afterwards, saying the sight of her had terrified him more than the memories she had freed. She hadn't appreciated his attempt to lighten the mood at the time.

There was still a long way to go before she had freed all of his memories, but it was a start, and hopefully she would be able to free some good memories soon, ones that would give him back the better days he had passed with her.

He took hold of her hands and rubbed his thumbs over her wrists, teasing the inside of them and sending a shiver up her arms. He trailed his fingers upwards and his expression shifted, turning serious again.

Isadora looked down at the twin bands that encircled her forearms, ones that matched the new ones on his and concealed her from everyone but him.

"I'm safe." She twisted her hands and wrapped them around his forearms. They tensed beneath her fingers and she could feel the doubts in him, the fears he buried deep so she didn't see them, and the guilt he felt. "You didn't lead the Devil to me."

"Not yet anyway," he muttered.

Isadora released his arms and snaked hers around his neck, drawing him down to her. He bent at the knee, bringing his face level with hers, and she sighed at the hurt in his eyes, at the thoughts she knew tormented him, fears that were unfounded. The Devil couldn't use him against her. Rook wasn't his to command, which meant he couldn't easily track where he was. The bastard was going to have to jump through the same hoops as the witches if he wanted to find them.

It didn't stop Rook from being protective of her. He hated letting her out of his sight, was her shadow whenever she wanted to take a walk, her escort whenever she uncovered the location of another spell book she desired, and her partner in crime.

And she kind of loved it.

Not that she was going to tell him that.

She smiled as he scooped her up into his arms and carried her into the cabin, kicking the door closed behind him.

"Where are we going?" Her heart fluttered, pulse racing at the way he held her close to him, his bare chest pressing against her side.

"Don't act coy." He grinned, lowered his head and nibbled her shoulder through her jumper. "Someone got me all fired up watching me chop wood."

She frowned when he turned right, away from the bedroom area of their cabin, and the heat flowing through her veins grew hotter as he stopped near the fire.

"I've wanted to do this for a long time." He kneeled, laid her down on the rug in front of the grey stone fireplace, and covered her with his body.

She moaned and arched up against him as he cupped her breast through her jumper, lightly squeezing it, and the thought of making love with him in front of the fire sent her temperature soaring.

Mother Earth, she was aching for him, wanted to caress and lick every inch of him, to worship his body and then have him worship hers.

She wasn't sure she could go slow though.

Was one hundred and ten percent certain she couldn't when he rose to kneel between her thighs and fingered the button of his black jeans, the firelight chasing over his muscles, accentuating them in a way that had that ache becoming a fierce demanding need.

The sexy tilt of his lips as he slowly popped the buttons, that self-assuredness that shone in his eyes as she hungrily devoured his body with her gaze, was her undoing.

She sat up, tore her jumper off and struggled out of her t-shirt, cursing when she couldn't remove them quickly enough.

His low chuckle warmed her.

So she was a little impatient. She wasn't the only one.

She tossed her tops onto the couch beside her and gave him a pointed look when she found he was naked before her now, his jeans vanished and his long hard cock jutting proudly towards her.

She groaned as he slowly fisted it, fell onto her back and wrestled with her jeans as that ache bloomed hotter inside her.

They disappeared too.

She did love that ability of his.

A moan bubbled up her throat as he covered her, his hips pressing between her thighs and cock rubbing her sensitive bead. She bowed against him and kissed him, claimed his mouth in a hard one because she couldn't hold back, was too far gone to care if he teased her about it later.

He was right.

The sight of him chopping wood was a weird kind of foreplay, but damn, nothing fired her up quite like it.

Nothing fired him up quite like it either.

Whenever she found him chopping wood, it always ended like this, with them tangled together, lost in each other.

She moaned into his mouth as he eased back and fed his cock into her, as he filled and stretched her, taking the edge off her need. She skimmed her fingers down his back, delighting in the feel of his muscles tensing beneath them, all that power at his disposal, strength he had used on her more than once.

"We ever going to do this thing slowly?" he murmured between kisses and she gasped as he began thrusting, curling his hips in long, urgent strokes that sent her flying higher.

"Not sure." She moaned and rocked in time with him, lowered her hand and clutched his backside as she wrapped her legs around him and used the heels of her feet to spur him on. "Like it like this."

He grunted in agreement, buried his face in her neck and sucked on it as he pumped her, clutching her hip to keep her in place.

Isadora jammed her heels into his bottom, making him go faster as she desperately reached for release, swore to herself they would take things slower in round two.

"Sweet fuck," he muttered and claimed her mouth again, kissing her deep and hard as he claimed her body.

He groaned and uttered a raw curse, broke away from her lips and pressed his forehead against hers, his breath washing across her face as he thrust into her, sending wave after wave of heat rolling through her that gathered in her belly as she moaned.

"Were we always like this?" He lengthened his strokes and if he thought she could hold a conversation while he was doing that, he was mistaken.

"No," she mumbled and tipped her head back as he shifted his knees, pushing her right leg up with his thigh and pumped her harder, hitting just the right spot. She gasped. "Yes."

"Which?" He grunted and groaned, shuddered in a way that said it felt damned good to him too, and muttered, "Never mind."

She giggled and gripped his shoulders, dug her nails in and clung to him for dear life as he took her higher. She couldn't hold on much longer.

"Fuck," he bit out and she moaned as he jerked deep into her, as he throbbed and scalded her with his seed.

A cry tore from her lips as the feel of him pushed her over the edge. Hot fiery sparks swept through her and she quivered, every inch of her trembling as bliss rolled over her.

Rook groaned and collapsed on top of her, breathing hard against her throat as he continued to pulse inside her and she throbbed around him.

Isadora sagged against the rug, her muscles turning liquid as she absorbed every drop of the pleasure he had given her and soaked up a little of what she could feel running through him too. She threaded her fingers through his hair, slicking the sweat-dampened strands back, and sighed.

"We started out gentler." She stared at the vaulted ceiling of the cabin, remembering those early days, and chuckled softly. "I think you were right..."

He lifted his head from her chest and frowned at her. "About what?"

"Sometimes it does pay to be a bad angel."

He slowly smiled, moved onto his elbows and pressed between her thighs. "Want me to show you just how bad I can be?"

That achy heat bloomed inside her again.

She wrapped her arms around his neck and lured him down to her. "Hell, yes."

He claimed her lips in a kiss that seared her.

Stamped his name on her heart all over again.

And as he held her close to him, the sense of peace that had been building inside her over the past few months crystallised into a feeling that stole her breath and that heart.

After a thousand years of being restless, of constantly moving, she was finally right where she belonged.

She was finally home again.

In the arms of her angel.

## *The End*

# ABOUT THE AUTHOR

Felicity Heaton is a New York Times and USA Today best-selling author who writes passionate paranormal romance books. In her books she creates detailed worlds, twisting plots, mind-blowing action, intense emotion and heart-stopping romances with leading men that vary from dark deadly vampires to sexy shape-shifters and wicked werewolves, to sinful angels and hot demons!

If you're a fan of paranormal romance authors Lara Adrian, J R Ward, Sherrilyn Kenyon, Gena Showalter, Larissa Ione and Christine Feehan then you will enjoy her books too.

If you love your angels a little dark and wicked, her best-selling Her Angel romance series is for you. If you like strong, powerful, and dark vampires then try the Vampires Realm romance series or any of her stand alone vampire romance books. If you're looking for vampire romances that are sinful, passionate and erotic then try her Vampire Erotic Theatre romance series. Or if you like hot-blooded alpha heroes who will let nothing stand in the way of them claiming their destined woman then try her Eternal Mates series. It's packed with sexy heroes in a world populated by elves, vampires, fae, demons, shifters, and more. If sexy Greek gods with incredible powers battling to save our world and their home in the Underworld are more your thing, then be sure to step into the world of Guardians of Hades.

If you have enjoyed this story, please take a moment to contact the author at **author@felicityheaton.com** or to post a review of the book online

**Connect with Felicity:**
Website – http://www.felicityheaton.com
Blog – http://www.felicityheaton.com/blog/
Twitter – http://twitter.com/felicityheaton
Facebook – http://www.facebook.com/felicityheaton
Goodreads – http://www.goodreads.com/felicityheaton
Mailing List – http://www.felicityheaton.com/newsletter.php

**FIND OUT MORE ABOUT HER BOOKS AT:**
**http://www.felicityheaton.com**

Printed in Great Britain
by Amazon

59248346R00092